JOHNNY
TUMBLED
DOWNWARD...

and spread his arms and legs wide as would a parachutist. The ground seemed to take its time moving up to meet him, but Johnny didn't care. Then there was softness and he was no longer falling. He hadn't flamed on. He hadn't landed. Where was he?

His arms jutted out and felt a plastic softness all around him. He was encased in something, but what?

What the hell was going on?

He jerked back and forth, trying to rip through the softness that held him prisoner, but he was unable to lift his arms. They fell heavily to his side as his legs crumpled under him.

He fell to his knees, asleep, quiet as a babe—and just as helpless.

Doctor Doom smiled. The last of the Fantastic Four was now his captive. And soon, they would all be dead. . . .

DOOMSDAY

BY
MARV WOLFMAN

Packaged and edited by
Len Wein and Marv Wolfman

PUBLISHED BY POCKET BOOKS NEW YORK

Another *Original* publication of POCKET BOOKS

POCKET BOOKS, a Simon & Schuster division of
GULF & WESTERN CORPORATION
1230 Avenue of the Americas, New York, N.Y. 10020

ISBN: 0-671-82087-7

First Pocket Books printing May, 1979

10 9 8 7 6 5 4 3 2 1

Trademarks registered in the United States and other countries.

Printed in the U.S.A.

To my father, Abe, who started me out. And to Michele and Jessica, who are continuing me on my trek.

1

Ben Grimm tore open the wide envelope with the thick, brickish stumps that passed for his fingers. His bright blue eyes sparkled for a moment as he read the printed announcement. "Brush my teeth an' call me Smiley! I don't believe this."

Lifting his massive body from the heavy iron chair especially constructed for him, he stomped out of the recreation room and headed for the private high-speed elevator which would take him to the thirty-seventh-floor lab where Reed Richards was undoubtedly hard at work on some new invention.

Ben grunted. Reed always had his long nose into something, and he was sure today would prove no different.

The elevator door shuddered as it reached the thirty-seventh floor, and the chrome-steel door slid noiselessly open. Ben stepped from the elevator and glanced at the lab door at the far end of the long blue corridor. His heavy footfalls echoed with every plodding step.

"I ain't been back there in years," he muttered to himself. "It'll be a blamed gas!" He was standing before the laboratory door now as he passed his hand over the electric-eye beam which would auto-matically activate and slide it open.

He entered, craning his neck in an attempt to find Reed Richards. "Hey, Stretcho, lay yer peepers on this. Ya ain't gonna believe it." Suddenly he heard Reed shouting at him. Something was wrong. Reed was in trouble.

"Ben! Get over here fast! We've got a rip in the Negative Zone couplings! It could blow at any moment!"

Instantly, Ben whirled, stabbing his massive hand at the emergency signal on the wall behind him. Sue and Johnny had to be alerted. Their powers would be needed if—

Ben leaped toward the far end of the lab when he heard the soft hissing whistle. He saw his friend struggle to brace a heavy steel plate over the Negative Zone door. Ben's lumbering body moved with surprising speed for a man almost as wide as he was tall. In a moment he was at Reed's side, his legs, which were thick as tree stumps, spread wide and firm for support. Ben pressed his powerful shoulders against the door as Reed stretched a long arm toward the opposite wall.

"You've got to hold it, Ben. We can't let it ex-plode." Reed's voice was filled with dread; the last time the Negative Zone door had opened, Reed had almost lost his life in the hideous dimension that existed on the other side.

"Then do somethin', high-pockets." Ben's wide mouth was distorted with pain. "It ain't holdin'. I can't keep 'er still. It's shakin' like a belly dancer's navel."

But Reed had already stretched back to his friend's side, his long fingers gripping the handle of an acetylene torch. Then, from behind them both, came a youthful voice. "Forget that, Reed. *I'm* here."

The master scientist turned to see Johnny Storm standing in the doorway, poised for action. Reed's wife, Sue, stood behind her younger brother.

"Reed! What happened?" she cried out, then ran to her husband's side. Sue then saw Ben straining at the Negative Zone door and quickly understood. "Johnny, you've got to do something fast!"

But Reed shook his head violently. "Get back, all of you. That terrible vortex could draw us all to our dooms. Get out, seal off this floor."

Johnny Storm gave a hurried smile. "No way, brother-in-law. Your acetylene flame isn't any match for the Human Torch. *FLAME ON!*" As he shouted, his flesh shimmered, then exploded with flame which spread instantly over his entire body. He pushed passed Reed and grabbed the heavy steel plate Ben was pressing to the door. "This is gonna get hot, blue-eyes. Think you can stand it?"

Ben grunted his answer. "Ain't nothin' you can dish out that I can't take, ya hot-headed little twirp. G'wan, use yer blasted flame an' don't worry none about the ever-lovin' Thing."

Johnny grinned for a moment, then increased the intensity of his flame as he slowly began to melt the doorway back in place. He and Ben had been arguing back and forth ever since the Fantastic Four had been formed, but they both loved each other as if they were brothers.

Sue Richards gripped her husband's arm; her eyes mirrored the fear she felt growing in her stomach. Ever since they had become the Fantastic Four she knew they constantly risked death. But she had always envisioned their deaths resulting from some great battle to save humanity from an awesome foe. She had never given thought to their dying because of mere steel couplings that should have been replaced months ago which would tear down the barrier between their dimension and the terrible darkness of the Negative Zone. This would be a wasted end . . . a horribly wasted death.

Though she was frightened her voice was quiet and firm. "Reed, can Johnny do it in time? Is there a chance?"

Reed shook his head. "I don't know, Sue. If Ben can keep the steel plate from slipping, and Johnny can weld it to the door quickly enough, we stand a good chance of making it."

It took less than a moment for all of Reed's hopes to be shattered. The steel crumpled like cardboard in Ben's hands, and the lab room was suddenly bathed in a sickly, unearthly, blinding green light.

Glass test tubes and slides flew across the room toward the yawning hole beyond the portal. Reed shouted over the awful roar. "Grab something— anything! If you value your lives, you'll hold onto a steel support beam!"

Papers and books tumbled helter-skelter through the portal and then vanished into the greenness beyond. A massive chair jerked forward and crashed into Johnny Storm, who stood closest to the open portal, fighting to maintain a handhold on a bolted lab table. "Reed!" He screamed. "I'm losing my grip!"

Sue reached forward, her temple throbbed with pulsing energy. Invisible tongs stabbed from her mind and grabbed for her brother. "Hold on, Johnny. I've set up a force field to catch you."

The energy tongs snaked around Johnny's waist and held him firm, but Sue wobbled under the terrible pressure the Negative Zone was exerting.

"I'm not going to be able to hold you for long. Can't fight the vortex and keep you steady. Johnny, please try to grab something before it's too late."

Reed flattened himself against a wall, his pliable body stretched wafer-thin by the awesome pressure which held him in place. But he could still think, and instantly he formed a plan. "Ben, grab onto Sue and anchor yourself. Johnny, Sue's going to let down her force shield. Try to grab for safety any way you can." His eyes darted toward his three friends as they struggled to hear him. "Sue, when Ben has grabbed you, form the strongest force field you can to seal off the Negative Zone door. Hold it in place as long as you're able. You understand that?"

Ben Grimm nodded. "I ain't gonna let Susie go. Don'tcha worry, Stretcho."

At once he lunged for the young blonde-haired woman and grabbed her with his powerful four-fingered hand. His other hand darted toward the wall and his fingers dug through the reinforced steel to create a handhold. "Awright, Suzie, it's up ta you."

Her head throbbed with incredible pain as the vortex power increased with every passing moment. Raw, seething energy lashed out to draw her through the portal, to be lost forever in the Negative Zone that lay beyond.

A million needles pricked her flesh and distorted her usually perfect features. Her stomach heaved in agony as she struggled to banish the pain from her mind. She had to think clearly, precisely; otherwise, she would be unable to use her powers.

Form an energy wall, she commanded herself. *Form a damned energy blockade and cover the Negative Zone. It's our only chance. You've got to be able to do it.*

11

Once more her temple throbbed and an invisible force was unleashed. It spread over the doorway, layer upon layer, each reinforcing the previous one. Slowly, she felt the pressure ease off, and then she saw a frantic Johnny Storm collapse corpse-like to the floor. Her eyes grew wide with horror. "Johnny! God, no—*Johnny!*"

Reed's angry voice shook her from her horror. "Forget him, Sue. Keep focused on the energy door. That's your only mission. Keep up the force field. Don't allow the Negative Zone to smash through your energy barrier."

But her brother lay unconscious, perhaps dying, on the floor before her eyes. How could Reed subject her to this stress? Blood seeped from her lips where she had bitten herself during the confusion.

Reed stretched his elongated body toward the acetylene torch, then glanced up at Ben, who was staring in shock at Johnny's unconscious body. "Ben, I need you now. I've got to weld the door shut. It's only temporary, but Sue can't keep her shield in place much longer. You with me?"

Ben was uncertain what to do next, but Reed's voice was strong, firm. "Yeah, yeah, I'm with ya." He saw Sue staring at her brother's body, praying for some sign of life, and all the while concentrating to maintain her force field.

Reed curled around the torn and shattered lab and pointed toward a small closet door beneath the lab table. "In there, Ben—you'll find a reinforced steel support plate. We'll use it to replace the shattered door. Hurry! Sue's weakening."

"Got it, Mister. What now?" Ben saw Sue's legs wobble for a moment, then tense. *Poor kid, she's dyin' inside ta be next ta Johnny now, but she knows Reed's right. We gotta perfect the Zone door. That comes first.*

12

"All right, Ben. Hold it over the opening. I'll use the torch; then Sue can release her shield. The door should hold until I can construct a permanent replacement."

Fifteen agonizingly long minutes passed before Reed Richards could look up from the door. "All right, Sue," he said softly, "release your shield, but stay ready. If our support isn't strong enough, we'll know it in a moment."

The replacement held firm, and Reed let out a long, deep breath, then rushed to Johnny's side. Sue was already over her brother, her small, delicate fingers on his muscular chest. "How is he, Sue? He's alive. He's got to be alive." Reed's voice was intense, filled with deep concern.

Saying nothing, Sue nodded. Then: "I—I think he's just stunned. I don't feel any broken bones, and his pulse is almost normal." She reached out for Reed's hand and held it firm for support. Then she stood and Reed brought her to him. Her head buried itself in Reed's chest.

"It's all right, honey. You can cry if you want to. I think we all need the release. It's been one helluva morning."

With a sharp pain, Johnny Storm opened his eyes to see a blinding light shining at him. Instinctively, he shut his eyes again. "Hey, what's going on here? Shut off that blasted light, will ya?"

Slowly, he opened his eyes a second time and he saw Reed hunched over him, the light in his hand now pointed away from the blond-haired Johnny Storm. "Reed? Wh-what happened? Where am I?" He knew the answer even before Reed could reply. He was in his private room on the thirty-fourth floor of the Baxter Building.

"You'll be fine now, son. Just take it easy for the day." Reed smiled as he stood up.

Ben Grimm plodded over to his side. "Bah, I shoulda known the pipsqueak would pull through. He's like a stubborn jackass. An' here I hadda waste five bucks buyin' 'im a book ta read while he wuz gettin' better. What a waste o' hard-earned bread."

Johnny grinned. "Consider it money well spent, Ben. Now you can curl up with it and have someone read it to you."

Ben lunged forward, his powerful arm reached out, and he grabbed Johnny's shirt. "I hope yer smilin' when ya say that, match-head. 'Cause if ya ain't, I'm liable ta ferget that yer weak an' sickly. Know what I mean?"

Johnny faked an anguished pout. "Oh, you can see I'm just terrified for my life. The big, orange, walking and talking brick wall is threatening me. Oh, woe is me."

Sue glanced at Reed. "I guess everything's back to normal. Those two are fighting again." Reed nodded. "They aren't happy unless they can tear each other down. I'll never understand them."

Then Ben looked up and removed a wide envelope from the blue swimtrunks that he wore. "I almost fergot; this came fer us, Stretcho. I think ya'll get a kick outta it."

Reed read over the printed invitation and a slight smile crossed his lips. *"You are cordially invited to attend your gala class reunion at Empire State University.*

"Lord, I haven't been back there in years. Sue, we haven't anything scheduled, have we?" Sue shook her head no.

"Class reunion . . . so much has happened since

14

those days that it almost seems like an eternity and not just a few years."

Ben nodded. "Ya better believe it, Stretcho. Since those days, ya became a big-brained scientist and conned us inta takin' yer cockamamie rocket fer a ride inta outer space."

Ben's thoughts drifted to that day, many years back. "I told ya yer shieldin' wuzn't gonna be strong enough ta keep out the cosmic rays, but ya wouldn't lissen. Now look at what those cosmic rays did ta us.

"It turned Susie into a blasted Invisible Girl whenever she wants ta pull a disappearin' act; it made the kid here a Human Torch, an' ya can stretch like ya was a walkin', talkin' rubber band. As fer me . . ."

Ben paused; his deep, rumbling voice became lower, softer. "It turned me inta this orange monster. Sheesh, I tell ya, Mister, at least ya three look human. I look like the underside of a brick wall."

Ben was taller than Reed, towering almost six and a half feet. His flesh had become coarse, hard, orange, brick-like blocks. He had no hair on his massive, craggy head. No hair and no ears. His brick brow was ridged and jutted over his round blue eyes. His mouth was a long obscene slit across his grotesque face.

He had a huge barreled chest which was also crag-like. His impossibly broad shoulders had massive stanchion-like arms growing from them. His hands were huge and three-fingered with a thick stubby thumb. His legs were thick columns with a four-toed foot at each end.

For all intents and purposes, Ben Grimm had become a monstrous hulking Thing, and Thing was what he caustically called himself.

But Reed Richards wasn't thinking of the cosmic accident which had created The Fantastic Four. He thought of school, and of one student in particular.

He thought of Victor Von Doom, and without thinking, he shuddered.

2

No trumpets sounded the day he was born. He was, after all, merely a Gypsy's son, someone to be shunted away, hidden in some dark corner to be forgotten. He would undoubtedly become a beggar or a thief if he didn't die young in some senseless squabble.

Yet, sharp-eyed Boris the lame saw the fire blazing deep in the infant's dark, brooding eyes, and only Boris noticed that when Gretchyn, midwife to Cynthia, laid her bare palm to young Victor's rear, the child did not cry.

And again, only old Boris realized the hour of the child's birth was the hour of the howling wolf.

Boris bowed to his young master. He would serve as vassal to Victor Von Doom. For now. Forever.

Werner Von Doom proudly sat at his wife's side as she nursed their newborn son. "Victor has your eyes, Cynthia," he said, "your shining, coal-dark eyes." He shuddered as the winter smoke curled from his lips.

Cynthia didn't smile; she rarely did. "I ache, Werner. Do you have your herbs?" Werner nodded quietly and reached for his bag. He was a Gypsy healer, perhaps the best in Latveria, and his bag of potions and herbs was always at his side.

"Drink this, my wife," he said, his deep voice echoing concern and fear. Cynthia did as her husband said, and the potion tasted bitter on her tongue. But she had tasted worse, much worse. Her own brews tasted of death.

Werner turned toward old Boris as his wife quickly fell asleep. "Let us leave. She needs her rest." Boris said nothing as he stepped from the tent. It was too late for words. Victor Von Doom lived, and he knew it was only a matter of time before the world would come to fear this Gypsy's son.

The boy was eight and studying at the foot of a master tutor from another village when Boris rode into camp, his aged face taut with fear. He shouted, "Victor! You must come home now. The Baron's soldiers have come to seize your father!"

The boy's expressionless face did not change. Quietly, he mounted Boris's horse. "Go, then. Hurry to my father's side. He will need me."

The child speaks like a man, Boris thought. *His heritage becomes more evident with every passing day. Soon it will be impossible to hold him back. Soon he will realize his tremendous power, and then* . . . Boris shuddered at the thought.

The soldier was clearly impatient. "Well, Gypsy, do you come with me now, or will you die?" Werner stared up at the soldier standing in the opening of his tent. "I am only a Gypsy healer. I've done nothing. I treat the sick and the suffering, that is all."

The soldier grunted. "Silence!" he commanded, his voice plainly thick with disgust at speaking with a lowly Gypsy. "You are to come with me by order of the Baron."

Werner rose, hatred burning in his eyes. *The one who killed my darling Cynthia was dressed in your colors, swine. I will never forget that.* He slung his medicine bag over his shoulder and thought of his wife. *Has it been six years since you were taken from me? I feel the pain and agony of an eternity.*

Werner mounted the old nag outside his tent when he saw Victor running toward him. "Father, what is happening?"

Werner Von Doom allowed a slight smile. "Do not worry, Victor. I have done no wrong. I will not be harmed."

"But the tribes need you, Father. *I* need you."

Boris limped to the young one's side. He placed a firm hand on Victor's shoulder. "Do not fear for your father, Victor. He will be safe, and I will look after you until his return."

Werner lifted the boy and held him tightly, then lowered him to the ground and rode off. "Why are they taking him, Boris? He only wishes to help the helpless. Why are they now after him?" Victor was confused, but his grim-set face reflected only bitter hatred.

Sadly, the elder Gypsy shook his head. "He is a Gypsy, boy—as are we all. It is a price we must pay."

The Baron sat in a plush velvet chair in the center of a magnificent banquet hall. He was a big man, powerfully built. A long dueling scar split his face from his left eye to his chin. "My wife is sick, Gypsy. Heal her." It was not a request. It was an order.

Werner shook his head. "Baron, it is hopeless.

It is beyond my power to save her. The grip has taken hold of her and will not let go."

The Baron's face grew red. "You lie, Gypsy. Use your magic potions to save her, or you'll pay with your own miserable life."

Werner shrugged his shoulders. He was doomed. The woman would die within three days and he would then be slain. Unless . . .

On the second day, a tired Werner Von Doom entered the Baron's throne room. "There is nothing more I can do, Excellency. She will recover."

"Go, then, Gypsy, and pray for your sake that you have been successful." With that, Werner was dismissed, and he quickly mounted his horse and rode off.

Night came early, and the castle was dark, save for a flickering candle in the Baroness's chamber. The nurse who held her lady's hand sang softly to herself, whiling away the night. Then she noticed the hand had become cold and limp, and her lady's eyes were clear and empty. The Baroness was dead.

By week's end, the Gypsy camp was overrun with the Baron's soldiers. "I want the healer," he demanded. "A boon to the man who brings his head to me." But Werner Von Doom and his young son, Victor, were long gone.

They fled into the night, taking to the snow-deep Alps. The thin winter coats Werner had grabbed were hardly warm enough to ward off the storm that was brewing.

"Why do we run like cowards, Father? We can stay and fight." Werner closed his lips to the freezing snows which blanketed him.

"You are like your dead mother. She, too, feared nothing, no matter how hopeless the odds."

But Victor was insistent. "We can beat them, Father. We have the power. There is nothing that can stop a Von Doom. Nothing!"

So proud, little Victor, so very proud . . . and so very foolish. There are forces frail men cannot fight. Werner sorely wished Cynthia was at his side to counsel him now.

They found a cave for sanctuary from the raging snows, and Werner huddled closely to Victor to keep the child warm. The night would be the death of them both, he felt, struggling to force open his eyes. But the fight was lost.

Soon dreams came.

Cynthia stood beside her caldron, her dark eyes blazing like the fires of Acheron. "I pass on my legacy to my son, Victor," she proudly sang. "All that I am, he, too, will be."

Werner watched helplessly as she placed the infant Victor into the heated caldron. The child refused to cry as the boiling herbs bathed his tender flesh. Then Cynthia smiled the smile of the wicked. "It is done. He is one with me."

The vision shifted. The Baron's troops thundered into the village. "Heretics! Blasphemers! Witches, all of you! Die! Die! *Die!*" The soldiers were mad that dark night. They cut the canvas of Von Doom's tent and tore Cynthia from his arms. He tried to help her, but a long sword was held to his throat, and he was forced to watch as his wife was ignobly drowned before his horrified eyes.

Eyes glazed over with sweat, he suddenly awoke. At his side, young Victor was still asleep, shivering from the bitter cold. Then, from outside the cave, he heard a whinny and the sound of galloping hooves.

21

"No! *No!*" Victor awoke as his father shouted into the grayness outside the cave. "What is it, Father? Have the Baron's troops found us?"

Von Doom's voice was one of defeat. "We have lost our horse, Victor. The ropes must have loosened during the night. We are as good as captured."

Victor shook his head grimly. "No. We won't surrender. No matter what happens to us, we will go on. A Von Doom never surrenders. A Von Doom is always victorious."

Tears streamed from Werner's eyes. *So much like his mother.*

For three days they plodded through the snows, shivering, teeth chattering with every step. They'd never make it, Werner thought. They would die. Then he would be at his wife's side again.

On the fourth day, they collapsed from fatigue and hunger. *Why go on? Let death take us now . . . let us go to our reward.*

Boris stared at the two lying at death's door. Werner was failing; he wouldn't last much longer. Young Victor was still unconscious, but breathing. He nodded toward a young girl to put two more logs on the fire. It was luck he had found them before the Baron's men did. But was he too late?

It took four days for Victor to be roused. The child was weak, emaciated, yet he insisted on being at his father's side. For a moment, Werner's eyes opened and he saw Victor's frail face staring down at him. "Heed my last words . . ." he sputtered out. "You must protect . . . protect . . ." And then nothing.

Victor fell to his father's side, his face grim.

22

"Father, no one will have to protect me. I shall become strong! Powerful! I will avenge your death!"

Yet Boris knew, for he alone remembered the Baron's purge so many years before. *He did not mean to protect you, young Victor. He meant the world must be protected . . . from the child who bears the name Von Doom.*

Boris turned toward his men. "Take away Werner's body. A funeral must be arranged." But Victor would hear nothing of it.

"They murdered my mother when I was but an infant. And now they have slain my father. They'll pay for that. All of mankind will pay." He was a snarling lion, but Boris quieted him with a glance.

"Victor, you are on your own now. These are your father's herbs and remedies. Use them only for good, lad."

Boris left and Victor was soon alone. "They'll all pay, Father. Mankind will be taught a lesson. I swear it."

He opened the trunk carelessly. "Your medicine trunk will no longer be needed, Father. I will not doctor the ill. I'll not spend a lifetime helping others only to suffer in the end."

Beneath the herbs and potions, he saw a small chest. Across its lid was his mother's name. "This belonged to her? I've never seen it before. What is it?"

The lid was locked, but Doom's agile fingers quickly picked it open. Inside were strange vials, powders . . . magic potions. And a diary.

He read through the night. Each page was a treasure unto itself, for each page told of a magic spell, a dark secret known only to those now long dead.

Werner Von Doom had never told his son his

mother's secret, but Victor Von Doom knew it at last. His mother had been a witch, and he . . . he had inherited her dark and awesome powers.

Outside, the night grew thick with storm clouds, and thunder razed the heavens. The gods knew that from this moment forth, the world would never again be the same.

२८

"Von Doom, you are hereby sentenced to death for crimes against our people. Have you any last words?" The wide man stared at the tall figure of Victor Von Doom. *Damned Gypsy thief*, he thought, *you deserve this death and more for what you have done*.

Von Doom laughed and said nothing.

"Very well, then," the heavy soldier continued. "Guards! Take your aim . . . *fire!*"

Seven bullets slammed into the tall, proud figure. Seven bullets cut through yielding flesh. Yet, when the smoke cleared, Von Doom still stood. And, more—he spoke. "You shall all live to regret this. Victor Von Doom swears you all shall suffer."

One of the guards who had fired at Doom recoiled in horror. "I shot him. I know I did. How can he still live?"

Fearfully, they stepped closer to Doom, and it was then that the world first learned of Doom's awesome talents. The man they had shot was not a man at all, but a finely constructed robot whose intricate circuitry was far beyond the science of any other living man.

Doom was an absolute genius. Using his mother's sorcery, he had mastered science. And for years he plied his science toward trickery and deceit. He had become an outlaw, wanted by the Latverian Army, and then, when they thought they had finally captured the willy Gypsy, he turned out to be a lifelike mannequin.

His evil genius continued to grow. He launched a private war on the Baron and his soldiers, and when the Baron at last fell dead at Von Doom's feet, a truce was called. Victor Von Doom was no longer a hunted man.

He was twenty when the American came. "Master," Old Boris said, "a stranger wishes to see you."

Doom's brow furrowed. "A stranger? Very well, show him in."

The American smiled, hiding his nervousness. *So,* Doom silently chuckled to himself, *even a foreigner can sense my ultimate power. Good. Very good.* "What is it, man? I am busy."

The stranger was short, wearing a checked suit and tie, and thick horn-rimmed glasses. "Von Doom," he said, "I'm the Dean of science at Empire State University. We've heard some very interesting things about you. And, frankly, after seeing some of your work here, I, uh, I think my trip may have well been worth it."

"To the point, man. My time is important." Doom's eyes glared contemptuously at the stranger. He had heard Americans were weak-kneed fools. Were they all like this simpleton?

The American was stammering now, nervous before this demon-eyed youth. "I . . . I'm prepared to offer you a scholarship to my university. I'm sure you're interested, and we can—"

But Doom cut him off sharply. "Your laboratory has the latest equipment? I demand nothing but the best."

"It has."

Doom ignored him and turned toward Boris. "You will stay here with the others until I return." Then, turning back to the American, Doom added, "Let us go now. I wish to begin my work."

Empire State University was a large, sprawling campus with more than ten thousand students. But they didn't interest Doom; all he wanted were the laboratories.

One by one, he examined the many labs: biology, physics, geology, chemistry. They would do. He glanced at his hand-written notes and thought aloud, "It could work. It could very well work."

"Anything in particular, friend?" Doom turned toward the tall smiling youth leaning in the doorway of the lab. "I asked, does anything in particular work, or are you just thinking aloud?" The youth was Doom's age, and he had short-cut brown hair which was already graying at the temples. *Another mindless American dolt.*

"Uh, it's just that it looks like someone else is as anxious to use the labs as I am. My name's Richards. Reed Richards." He extended a hand.

Doom picked up a slide and placed it under the microscope. "That is of no concern to me. Leave me alone."

Richards let out a long, low whistle. "Look, I don't know why you've got this king-sized chip on your shoulder, but being we're both here on scholarship, how about us rooming together?"

"I have no wish to share a room with anyone," Doom said, his voice sharp and final. "I demand privacy! Good-bye."

Reed Richards shook his head, smiling, though exasperated. "Well, it's none of my business, but aren't you carrying this 'mad scientist' bit a little too far? I only offered friendship."

Shoving the microscope aside, Doom stood up. "Men always think their superiors are mad. Now leave—this moment. I have no wish for further conversation—now or at any other time."

"Whatever you want, pal. It's fine with me." Richards was almost pleased he had been rebuffed. There was something ominous about Doom.

Leaving the Latverian, Reed roomed with another man, a big, burly football hero named Benjamin Grimm. As they became fast friends, Doom stayed alone, hidden in his laboratory.

Months flew by; classes were cut. But nothing mattered to Doom save his experiments. Not even Dean Collins could speak to the Latverian student with the delusions of grandeur. "See here, Doom," Collins had told him, "you're a student. I have no use for foul-tempered children. You will conform to university regulations, or . . ."—he let his voice drop for effect—". . . or you will leave. Is that understood?"

Doom said nothing. For the moment, he needed the university and its equipment. And if it meant mollycoddling this base inferior, so be it. With an arrogant gesture, he spun and strutted out of the office and returned to his laboratory. He would have to speed up his work and then get out.

The door to his lab was ajar. Inside, a small desk lamp silhouetted the tall figure of Reed Richards hunched over an open ledger. Doom's temper flared. "What are you doing here, cretin?"

Calmly, Richards turned. "Just wanted to say hello and see how you're doing. You're into some heavy material, Doom. Matter transmutation and dimensional warping. Interested in working with a partner? I've got my own theories on Negative space that—"

Doom cut him off. "I told you before, lout, Victor Von Doom works *alone*. Now, get out of here, or next time I see you I shall make you regret having come here."

"Just trying to be friendly. By the way, you'd better double-check some of these equations. You're a few decimal points off."

Doom's voice cut like thunder in the night. "Give me that! Now, get out! Get out this instant!"

Reed handed Doom his ledger and left, shutting the door behind him. No use in trying to befriend that maniac.

The reconstructed laboratory was behind his room; the newly built machinery was humming as usual. In the center of the darkened room sat a heavy steel-gray chair, wires and metal tubing lining its sides. Von Doom smiled. *What could that fool know of equations? I am Victor Von Doom! I do not make mistakes!*

"Von Doom?" The frail voice came from the shadows. The thin, blond-haired assistant stepped forward. "Von Doom, I fixed up your gadget the way you wanted, but I still don't like it."

"Yours is not to question me, dolt! Do as you are told!" Arrogantly, he strode toward the chair and sat heavily in its iron seat. He glanced toward the blond-haired man, who twitched fearfully as Doom stared at him.

"If the faculty staff ever learns that you've been conducting forbidden experiments, trying to contact the nether world—" He shook his head sadly.

"Those cretins will learn nothing, fool. By tomorrow my experiments will be done." Doom gestured toward the red-painted lever on the computer console facing him as he lowered a clear plastic dome over his face. "You will throw that switch now. It is time! *Now!*"

"But—?"

"*Now!*"

Doom almost grinned, but he quickly clenched his jaws. *My dreams will now become reality.* His mind wandered to his mother: *She dared to risk the infinite. She dared to challenge the universe. She—*

A single corruscating moment almost ended all of Doom's dreams forever. There was a flash of intense light, and a heart rending explosion. It tore through the laboratory walls and shattered glass everywhere throughout the campus.

The lab was a smoky ruin; chrome-steel computers were reduced to twisted lumps. Yet, somehow, miraculously, Doom still lived.

His bones were crushed, his face torn and mangled, yet he didn't cry—not when he was dragged from his lab little less than dead, not when surgeons labored over him month after month refitting bone, grafting skin and tissue, applying new medicines never before used.

He lay helpless in bed for months longer, never speaking, never divulging what successes or failures his experiments had had.

Six months passed before he could move. And then his progress was astonishing. One day he was paralyzed; the next day he could walk. Doctors certified he would never again speak, that his vocal cords were frozen. Then, in a thick, heavy voice that sounded like roaring cannons, he'd order those same doctors to leave him alone.

Seven months to the day of the explosion, Dean Collins entered the darkened hospital room. The shades were drawn; only a small candle provided light.

"What do you want, Collins?" Doom demanded.

"To tell you that I am expelling you from school. You're uncontrollable, Doom—a menace to us, and a menace to yourself. I'll not put up with it any longer."

For perhaps the first time in his long, grim life, Doom laughed. "There is nothing more you dolts can teach me, anyway. You had outlived your usefulness long before the accident occurred. Now, get out! If I ever see you again, I swear you shall feel my unending wrath!"

4

𫝀𫝀𫝀𫝀𫝀𫝀𫝀𫝀𫝀𫝀𫝀𫝀𫝀𫝀𫝀𫝀𫝀𫝀𫝀𫝀𫝀𫝀𫝀𫝀𫝀𫝀𫝀𫝀𫝀𫝀𫝀𫝀

It was almost winter before the bandages were removed and in a mirror he saw the hideous mockery his face had become. His flesh was torn and scabbed, his hair missing and clumped in disgusting patches. Deep scars traced his face like the lines on a roadmap, and it was more than the proud Victor Von Doom could stand.

"God, I'm ugly—disgustingly ugly!" he cried, tears burning the welts that pockmarked his face. "What have I done to myself? What?"

A powerful fist smashed the mirror into a thousand cursed reflections, and blood ribboned down his torn hand. "It is too disgusting, too horrible. No other eyes must ever see my face again."

He took to Asia and the mountains of Tibet. His mother's diary told of an unknown sect of monks whose mastery of the Dark Arts made Cynthia's knowledge pall in comparison.

The winter was especially harsh, bitter winds whipped around every peak, and Doom could only curse the gods for the freezing temperatures and the foul game that occasionally dared the icy snows. But Doom pressed on, remembering another wintry trek he had made with his father. He refused to be defeated then; nothing could stop him now.

The snow blinded him and for days he plodded forward, never knowing if his next step would take him toward his destination, or plunge him into a deadly crevasse.

His throat was parched, his muscles ached, and his bare skin would be cut and blood would instantly freeze to the wound. Hunger drove him mad and demons plagued his nights, yet nothing could stop him. He was Victor Von Doom. He would continue.

Until he dropped.

The snow was a warm blanket that gently covered his unconscious form. In his mind's eye, he saw the seashore and proud horses, and Gypsies singing around the campfire. He saw his tall father holding his medicine bag tightly to his chest, laughing with the others, singing his bawdy songs.

And when the festival seemed to be at its zenith, he saw only blackness and he knew he was dead.

They spotted him in the snow, his bandaged face buried in a high drift, his parka ripped beyond usefulness, his provisions gone.

Four of them lifted him and brought him to their cave to be warmed by the fire. One robed figure motioned to the other: *"Bring me the herbs and remedies."* He said nothing but was instantly understood. A third man removed his dark hood and sat cross-legged before the fire. The legends had foretold that one day "a faceless man will be your master." Surely this man whose features had been ravaged was the man they had been promised.

For two months Doom slept in a coma; his pains had been eased by these strange, silent monks who prayed to the Dark Gods for his recovery. On Walpurgis Night, the day of Doom's own birth, the fever which held him passed, and his eyes opened, and he picked himself off the straw cot and proudly stood before the monks, who bowed to him, chanting, "Master . . . master . . . master."

Doom was satisfied. He was home.

A month later, he was strong. "There is much for me to learn. Your dark sciences and your most ancient secrets must be mine." The monks bowed in acquiescence. They had awaited his coming for two thousand years. They were his to command.

By fall, there was nothing he did not know. He had mastered their sciences and sorceries with amazing ease. But something still nagged at him. The outside world had probably thought him dead. That insult could not be allowed. He had to return to life.

Then the awesome job began. Using the mouth of a giant idol as a makeshift furnace, the Gypsy son forged the most dreaded battle armor the world would ever see.

Within an unshatterable steel shell, he molded every weapon his mad mind could conceive. His servants took careful measurements: the arms, the legs, the chest . . . they all had to perfectly fit Von Doom.

Intricate computer circuitry was placed in the heavy iron glove, and on the right index finger a small ring was hidden which would unlatch the dreaded mask . . .

. . . that great gray skull-like face that would cover Doom's own demolished visage.

"Does the armor pain you, Master?"

"Pain? That is for lesser men! What can pain mean to Victor Von Doom? Now—place on the mask!"

"But, Master, it has not completely cooled."

"Say no more, monk." Doom's voice was seething with anger. "I will tolerate no further delay. I cannot wait a moment more."

The great iron mask, still burning red with flame, was brought by heavy tongs toward Doom. His dark, brooding eyes glowed hungrily as it was placed on his face. "Never again will mortal eyes gaze upon the hideous countenance of Victor Von Doom. From this moment on, I shall be known as —DOCTOR DOOM!"

He stood tall and silent, a nightmare in gray, as a frightened monk approached him with the great green robe of Godhood, which he draped over Doom's powerful shoulders. Gold-spun cord held by two golden disks fastened the flowing cape in place.

Yet even as he stood proud and regal as a King, Doom knew this iron armor was not yet enough. He needed power . . . the power of a country . . . to give him the immunity he required for his total scheme to be realized. And what better land to rule than the simple Bavarian country of his birth.

He had fled Latveria as a frightened child. But he would return as its absolute Monarch.

Years passed, and Doom gazed out the castle window watching his subjects scurry like mice far below him. They accepted him as ruler as he knew they would. His power assured that simple fact.

They were his people, and he treated them well, and he made their land more prosperous than it had ever been before. He asked little of them except total blind obedience, and his robot guard patrol would assure that.

Doom had his country, but he still wanted more.

"Tomorrow is the date, Master," the old voice

informed him. Doom turned from the window toward ever-loyal Boris. "Tomorrow is the date, sire."

Doom's own voice was deep and rumbling. "Yes, tomorrow the first step in realizing my true destiny will be taken. Prepare for my journey to America, Boris. I wish to arrive fashionably late for the festival.

"And I wish to see Reed Richards's face when I do."

With that, Doctor Doom threw back his great iron-clad face and laughed a cold, bone-chilling laugh.

5

As he straightened his tie and stretched an arm into the jacket of his new blue suit, Reed Richards said, "Ready, Sue?"

"What do you think of this, darling?" Sue asked, leaning into the doorway of their Baxter Building apartment. She wore a gold strapless evening gown cut low in front and plunging to her waist in back. The shimmering gown hugged her perfect figure where it was supposed to, and Sue looked every inch the model she had been before she had met Reed.

Appreciative, Reed circled his slim wife and whistled. "You'll be the center of attention in that —dare I call it a dress? Is there enough material in it to legally call it a dress?" His eyebrow arched upward in mock seriousness.

Sue pouted. "Do you like it or not? And, please, don't leer. It just doesn't become an internationally known scientist such as yourself to leer so sala-ciously. After all, what if our son saw you like that?" She tsked him with a broad smile, then turned away with great flourish.

Reed crossed the room and took Sue into his arms. "I can ask the same, darling. Mothers didn't look like you when I was growing up."

He smiled a broad smile and lowered his voice to a whisper. "I don't think I've ever seen you lovelier: not when we first met; not when we got married. Maybe I'm going crazy, but as you get older you get more and more beautiful.

"You don't have an old painting aging in the closet by any chance, do you?" He laughed, then bent his head low to kiss her, not the mild kiss of a long-married couple familiar with each other, but the passionate kiss of a couple newly married, still anxious and fresh. It was long, fierce, and warm.

He felt her warm shoulder sway in his arms, and he was unable to remember ever caring about anyone before he had met her. Perhaps he had never even cared about himself.

He had always thought of himself as rather stiff and cold, all too logical. He had been raised in an orphanage and couldn't remember what it must have been like to be loved and to love someone else in turn.

Work was all he busied himself with: the logical doings of the mind, he always told himself. The endless limit of his imagination could extend itself, should extend itself. He submerged his emotions, thought about nothing but his work.

Then he had met Sue, and she was always warm and laughing. So much the opposite of himself, yet he was fanatically drawn to her—not so much for her subtle beauty, but for how she acted when they were together.

She would readily listen to his hopes and dreams, and somehow she would always say something that would spur him ever on. She understood little of his work, but she cared about what he did because she cared about the man.

Sue Storm was able to make you the whole of

her concern; nothing but you mattered while she was with you.

But she didn't live for you alone. She had her own full life. She had been a model and at one time her all-American face was featured on every woman's magazine. She was an actress who many considered a natural—"the new Hepburn!" the critics had called her. Her miraculous sensitivity somehow was reflected on the silver screen fifty times larger than life itself.

Yet she left the movies as unfulfilling. "I don't need to play-act," she said in one interview. "I have my own life I want to lead; I have things to do."

At a White House reception for the sciences, Sue Storm spotted a tall, awkward-looking man sitting quietly in a dark corner, scribbling on a paper napkin with a blunt pencil, obviously oblivious to the social function he was attending.

The man was somewhat handsome, his brown hair already gray at the temples. "Excuse me," she had said. "This seat taken? Your wife here?"

Reed Richards glanced up from his paper, somewhat confused. "Uh, no. I'm not married." His stare returned to the paper and he continued to scrawl a complex formula on the napkin.

She sat next to him. "Let's see, now. I take it you're not one of the caterers working out the cost for this party. Am I right?" Once again Reed glanced up, confused. She was smiling broadly, and he then realized she had been watching him for ten minutes as he wrote down the formula for a non-fossil fuel he was trying to develop.

Her smile was contagious. "I'm sorry, Miss. I didn't know I was being rude. It's just that I had thought of substituting an alcohol-base compound for—I'm doing it again, aren't I? I—"

"Don't apologize. I was bothering you. My

name's Susan Storm. . . ." He listened, not connecting the name, or perhaps he had never heard it before. He put out his hand and took hers. "Richards, Reed Richards. I'm with the institute."

"Well, do you like it or not? You still haven't said anything." Reed shook the cobwebs from his mind and grinned.

"Let me put it this way, Sue. If I had never known you before, I would fall instantly and madly in love. Yes . . . I like it. Does that make you feel better?"

Sue threw up her hands. "A romantic! I married a man as romantic as Swiss cheese. What did I ever see in you, Reed Richards?"

Reed shook his head, wondering. "I don't know, but if I ever find out, I'm going to package it and sell it as a guaranteed aphrodisiac. By the way, have you seen Ben and Alicia?"

"If ya didn't, ya just didn't look in the right places." Ben's gravelly voice boomed from behind them and they turned to see the orange-skinned Mr. Grimm dressed in an ill-fitting black tuxedo, a flourished white shirt, and absolutely no shoes at all. He looked like a bizarre grotesquerie created for a comedy film by Mel Brooks.

"Whadda ya laughin' about, Stretcho? Ya know it ain't easy ta find a tux in size two-hundred gorilla." Indignant, Ben looked at Alicia. "Ya believe the nerve o' them, kid? Sheesh, I tell ya, with friends like these . . ."

Alicia smiled. "I'm sure if I could see you, Ben, I'd probably have the same reaction. From how Reed describes you, you probably are a rather strange sight."

Ben grumbled. "Just 'cause I look like a monster, everyone's gotta pick on me—even my gal." Ben's voice seemed disturbed, but he knew better. Despite his gargoyle appearance, Alicia loved him—and not because she was blind and couldn't see his monstrous features.

Alicia was a sculptor, perhaps one of the best in New York. And her blindness only enhanced the empathic sensitivity her work displayed. She had created many statues of Ben in the years she had known him, and they all portrayed his strengths and virtues, somehow clearly apparent even over his seemingly brutish appearance.

She was the stepdaughter of one of the Fantastic Four's earliest foes, yet she loved Ben and his friends though they had to battle her father time and time again. If only her father, with his two sighted eyes, could see them as clearly as she could, blind.

Ben was sweet, gentle, kind, and giving, and there was something tragic about him that brought out her love even more.

He had been turned into something inhuman, his temper was at times ferocious, and his power was enough to level a city block with apparent ease, yet he could take a wounded bird in his thick, brick-like hands and shed a somber tear when the bird had died.

He may be a monster to some who can only see his thick orange skin, but he had more humanity in him than almost anyone Alicia Masters had ever known.

"Well, we leavin' or stayin'? I gotta get this monkey-suit back ta the shop by mornin'." Ben reached for a large cigar and stuck it in his wide mouth. "C'mon, I ain't got all day."

Sue turned toward the monitor screen and pressed for Johnny's room. "Hold on, I just want to say good-bye to Johnny." The viewscreen flickered

43

and Johnny's face appeared on it. "We're going, Johnny."

Her brother smiled. "Have a good time, Sis, and don't worry about anything here. Franklin's off with Agatha Harkness and I've got a date. Just enjoy yourself, okay, Sis?"

Sue nodded and flicked off the image. Agatha Harkness was their son's tutor and sitter, a strange woman who lived in an old mansion in upstate New York, in a place called Whisper Hill. When they hired her, they thought she would merely be a baby-sitter. They didn't learn until much later that she fit into their extended family better than they could have expected.

Agatha Harkness was a witch, and she was damned good at it.

6

ᘒᘒᘒᘒᘒᘒᘒᘒᘒᘒᘒᘒᘒᘒᘒᘒᘒᘒᘒᘒᘒᘒᘒᘒᘒᘒᘒᘒᘒᘒᘒᘒᘒᘒᘒ

"Reed Richards! My God, it's been years. How are you, lad?" Dean Collins had a broad smile as he shook Reed's hand. "You're our most famous alumnus, Reed. You don't know how pleased I am you came."

Reed smiled, happy to see the older man. Dean Collins had been his mentor throughout his four years at E.S.U. "I'm glad I could make it. You know my wife Sue, of course."

Sue Richards nodded at the retired Dean. "I'm happy to finally meet you, Mr. Collins. Reed has told me so much about you that I feel I know you personally."

Dean Collins took her hand and kissed it. "And you're even lovelier than your photographs picture you to be, my dear. Come, let me introduce you to some of the others."

Dean Collins led her into the large crowd of people milling about the bar. Reed smiled. *Retirement hasn't aged him one bit. Good for him.*

The room was a converted gymnasium, with the bleacher seats rolled back, decorations hung, and tables hastily set up with food and drink. A portable bar was manned by professional bartenders who carefully poured drinks for the joyous crowd. Reed estimated more than three thousand school-mates jammed the large gym.

Ben Grimm stiffly picked at his collar. "Sheesh, Collins didn't even give a hello. Ya think he didn't recognize me, Stretcho? Ya don't think I changed that much since college, eh?" Reed suppressed a growing smile.

"Dean Collins and I worked together for several years, Ben. He got me my first job with the Science Institute. You were here on an athletic scholar-ship."

"Sure, sure. He just didn't realize who I was, right? I mean, ya seen one orange-skinned mon-ster an' they all get ta look alike, don't they? Sheesh.

"Alicia, ya want me ta get ya a drink?" Alicia smiled sweetly. "Yer regular, babe?"

Ben plodded over to the bar, where several of his old classmates toasted one another. One of the women saw him first and gasped. "Oh, God, what is he? Look at him! He's a . . ." She couldn't say "monster" as Ben stared into her eyes.

"I'm the school nurse, blondie. Ya wanna make somethin' of it?" His coarse voice thundered in the woman's ears. Frightened, she backed away from him and clutched her husband's arm.

The man gulped in horror. He had to say some-thing. He had to protect his wife from the . . . the *thing* that stood no less than three feet from him. "Wh-why did you scare Madeline like that? She didn't do anything to you." His knees wobbled in fear. What would the creature do?

Ben turned to the bartender and ordered two vodka gimlets, then returned to see the small man quaking before him. "Lemme see, here, I was just

46

orderin' a couple o' drinks, an' yer old lady called me a monster. The way I see it, she's the one who scared me. Ya gotta understand, shortie, ta me, *yer* the monsters."

The man backed off a foot and tried to shake off his fear. "P-please apologize to my wife. Look at her." He puffed out his chest, regaining his lost courage.

Ben stepped closer to the man and stuck out a finger. It hooked the man under his collar, and effortlessly, Ben lifted him off his feet. "Tell ya what, baldie, how's about we both ferget this before ya make me real angry an' ya force me ta ferget this is supposed ta be a party. Understand?"

The room was silent now, all eyes turned toward Ben and his frightened adversary. Would there be a fight, even though everyone knew it would only last a fraction of a second?

Alicia spoke up. "Excuse me, Ben, I thought you were getting me a drink." Ben nodded sheepishly. It had been years since he had become the Thing. By now he should have been accustomed to the horrific stares his presence elicited.

"I was doin' just that, babe—then baldie, here, hadda go cause some trouble. Ya know me. I hate trouble." Ben ambled over to the bench where five rather heavyset men sat. "Don't get up," Ben said as he lifted the bench *and* the men with one hand.

"Ya know how I just shrivel up when trouble comes my way, babe. Anyway, he was just gonna apologize an' then we wuz all gonna go back ta havin' fun." Ben gently put the bench back in place. "Weren't ya, shortie?"

The man nodded. "I'm sorry. I won't bother you again. I promise." He looked back at his wife, glaring at him. Madeline would have to understand. He didn't want to find himself dismembered. Not this evening.

Ben smiled. "I knew ya'd see things my way, guy. Tell ya what, the drinks're on me. Awright?"

The man shook his head. "I'm giving up drinking. I don't want to touch this stuff again. In fact, I don't feel very well. I've got to go. C'mon, Madeline. We've got to go." He tugged at his wife's arm.

"But, Gregory, I—"

"We've got to go, dear. We're selling the house tonight and moving to another state . . . maybe another country. Uh, good-bye. Nice meeting you all. Madeline . . . c'mon. *Now!*"

They left Madeline confused. Then Ben turned toward the crowd. "I said the drinks were on me— at least the first dozen. C'mon."

Within moments, the joyous drone returned to the gymnasium. The band began its stirring rendition of "How Much Is That Doggie in the Window?" And voices could be heard everywhere. The minor distraction was all but forgotten.

For one hour, the party continued, couples danced, old acquaintances were renewed, business cards were exchanged, and phone numbers were traded along with mutual promises of getting together soon.

Old flames came upon each other, men meeting women they had loved and left, women introducing their current husbands to old boyfriends. Embarrassing stories were dredged up; school songs thought to be forgotten were remembered and sung out of tune.

It was ten-thirty when Reed noted a commotion at the gymnasium door. There were crowds of men and women streaming to the door. "Something's happening, Sue," Reed said. "I've got to see what's going on."

Sue held him back. "It's probably nothing, darling. Or maybe Ben's getting into another ruckus. C'mon, introduce me to that stunning redhead who's been giving you the eye all evening."

Reed shot Sue a strange stare. "What redhead? I didn't see anyone."

Sue smiled cunningly. "I bet you didn't. Confess, husband, was she an old girl friend you don't want me to know about? I'm not letting you off the hook so easily."

The commotion at the door continued. Then there was a hushed silence as Reed could hear Dean Collins's voice coming from the crowd. "I— I don't think you should come in here. You're not—" Collins's voice stopped abruptly.

It was replaced by another voice, a cold voice, one devoid of any emotion. It sounded harsh to the ear, rasping, as if it were mechanically filtered. "I was a student here, Collins. I demand entrance, and I will not be denied."

Reed recognized the voice instantly. He had heard it many times in the past, and each time it filled him with dread.

He stretched his neck to the gymnasium roof to peer above the crowd. It was *him*. His worst fear had been realized. Of all of Empire State University's students, *he* was not expected to show his presence here. Certainly not without fanfare. Indeed, Reed had not even known he was in the country.

The crowd parted, and the tall man entered. Then Sue let out a stunned gasp.

Majestically, powerfully, he stepped inside the gymnasium, knowing all eyes were now upon him, as well they should be.

The large hall seemed to shrink with the sudden and unexpected appearance of Empire State University's most infamous student . . . *DOCTOR DOOM—MONARCH OF LATVERIA!*

7

Ben was the first to react. His powerful fingers ripped off his shirt and jacket, leaving them tattered rags upon the polished wooden floor. His pants split along their seams and became more useless rags. Now Ben was clad only in the blue bathing trunks that were his action dress. He felt comfortable this way. Comfortable, and free to move.

He shouted; his voice boomed like cannon fire. "Ya lousy, slimy tin can! How dare ya smash yer way in here?" With powerful leaps, the brutish Thing was at Doom's side in an instant, and his massive hands grabbed Doom's iron armor, but the Latverian leader stood stiff and still.

"Take your monstrous hands off me, you oafish clod. How dare you defile a true Monarch with your disgusting touch?"

Ben's temper exploded, his right arm whirled back, and he formed a massive fist. "Ya tin-plated creep, I'm gonna make ya regret comin' here!"

Suddenly, through the crowd, Reed Richards stretched his snake-like body, his arms elongating, his fingers curling around Ben's fist. "No, Ben, don't. He hasn't started any fight. You can't strike him."

But nothing could stop Ben Grimm now. His fist flashed forward and pummeled the still-un-moving figure. "Monster, am I? Lemme show ya what kinda monster I am, tin-head!"

Ben clamped both hands together and whirled at Doom. The stiff figure rattled, and then his head jerked loose from his shoulders and flew across the suddenly silent crowd. "Whaa? I knocked off his blamed head. I don't believe it."

Ben stopped; his hands dropped like anchors to his side. His face took on a shocked expression. "I don't believe it. I didn't clobber 'im that hard. I know I didn't."

"Of course you didn't, you stupid, senescient fool. Do you truly believe Victor Doom would allow himself to be so easily defeated by a monster with the mind of an infant?" Doom stood in the doorway of the gym and lifted the robot body that Ben had crushed from the floor. "I knew my appearance here would cause such a brainless display of violence. And Victor Von Doom abhors such mindles reactions. Perhaps now that you have vented your brutish anger, you can go sulk like a whimpering pup in the corner."

"I clobbered a robot? That's what I smashed?" Ben was still amazed, although he knew Von Doom's evil genius could easily create an automaton far more elaborate than the one he had brought here.

Dean Collins stepped forward, pushing past Ben Grimm. "And you are still as arrogant as ever, Von Doom. I told you many years ago you were never to return here. That still has not changed."

Von Doom tilted his head quizzically at the small man. With but a minor display of power, he could incinerate this fool. But this was not the time and certainly not the place. He had achieved a minor victory by forcing the brutish Thing to react. Now it was his time to act . . . but with kindness.

Vengeance would come later.

"Dean Collins, I was once a student here, and it is my wish to attend this reunion. Please believe me, I have no wish to create trouble. I merely anticipated my presence here would create violence. My robot was designed to let it harmlessly pass, and then to continue celebrating the festivities."

Dean Collins fumed. "Doom, I don't like you. I never have, and I do not care if you did attend this school. I don't wish you to be here now. Leave, or I'll call for the police."

Doom laughed and saw Reed Richards standing behind the crowd, his arm around his wife's waist. "Richards, tell the man that would be a wasted gesture. As Monarch of a foreign nation, I have certain immunities from your law officials. Besides which, I have done nothing but attend a party open to all my fellow classmates."

Reed was grim. Doom was right. Even if they could have him removed, which was doubtful, he could not be prosecuted. He enjoyed diplomatic immunity, and Doom used that immunity with pleasure.

"I'm sorry, Dean Collins, but we can't do anything—not unless he attacks us first."

Collins let out a low curse. "Damn it, Doom, so help me, if you try anything . . ." He sputtered, not being able to think of anything he could do to the younger, vastly more powerful man who stood arrogantly before him.

Ben stared at Alicia. "He's playin' some sorta game, babe. It ain't like him ta play party."

Alicia tightened her grip on Ben's arm, and she

spoke softly. "He is an evil man, Ben. . . . his voice is harsh and wicked, and he talks with an arrogant attitude. He feels himself better than any man here. Please, Ben, don't antagonize him. There is no depth to which he will not sink to destroy an enemy."

With long strides, Doom stepped to the center of the room. Still nobody spoke. *The utterly contemptible fools. Look at them, struck silent at my mere appearance.*

"I have come here," he announced, "to offer forgiveness to this university for its rash treatment of me. I understand my actions had caused them some minor grief. Indeed, it destroyed the face beneath this iron mask, so I, too, have suffered for my, ah, sins. But I am here in the presence of my former friends to end the bitterness that stands between us all. I offer a gift few men have ever been given. My castle and all its wonders and glories are yours. I propose that this celebration be moved to my home in Latveria, where you common people will be permitted entrance into the grandest of all the European empires. You will be personally escorted on a tour of my home, and you will be safely returned here Sunday night.

"There is no trick in what I offer. I guarantee your safety—and more, I guarantee you will all be well rewarded for your journey. You will see sights no American has ever seen before. You will witness the wonders of Latveria, and its proud people, who serve me so zealously.

"I offer this all to you, my friends, as a tribute to this university. Without my brief time spent here, I would not be a ruler among rulers today.

"To assure everything I say is true, I invite Reed Richards and his friends to join us. Surely their great power will guarantee that I mean you no harm.

"I have a fleet of my royal jets awaiting us at the airport. We will arrive in Latveria before noon. Tomorrow and Sunday are yours, a gift from your humble fellow student. What say you, my friends?"

Doom's impassioned speech brought stunned silence. How to answer? Voices murmured in whispers between husbands and wives. *A European trip, free? But what if he attacks us? But Reed Richards will be there. He wouldn't dare do anything. How can we say no? Think of it: we'll never be offered a personal tour of a royal palace again. Please, say yes. I want to go.*

Ben Grimm stood firm. "I don't know what yer up ta, Doom, but I don't like it. Count me out."

Reed Richards shook his head. "I agree, Doom. You've never made any effort toward benevolence before. What are you up to?"

Doom was waiting for this; indeed, he had prepared for this very speech. "Up to? My dear colleague, I invite you to join us. Would I do that if I were up to something? Bring along your wife and friend. I want to make amends for our previous encounters.

"I see you do not believe me, Reed Richards. Very well, tell me what I must do to prove I have changed my ways. I no longer wish to expand my power. Indeed, I have decided that little Latveria is enough for any one man to rule.

"I merely wish to benefit mankind from this day forth. If you come with me, I will throw open the door to my many scientific secrets. They will be made available for all mankind to study.

"What else do you want from me, sir? I capitulate, I offer no resistance, should you wish to battle and destroy me now. I have no weapons on me or hidden in my invincible armor. Search me if you wish. You will see I speak the truth."

"Don't do it, Stretcho," Ben said. "He's up ta somethin' stinkin'. I can smell it."

Yet Reed was unsure. Doom's science was magnificent. To have it revealed to mankind would prove a terrific boon. "I will come wtih you, Doom, to safeguard these people and to see if what you say is true. But I won't force Ben or Sue to join us, and if anyone else decides not to come, I want them to be able to leave here now, unharmed. Is that clear?"

"It is clear, my friend. Very clear." Doom spoke without emotion, but he felt elation. *The fools believed me. How easy it is to offer peace. How quickly they grasp at any straws of hope. And how devastating they will find it when they are instantly and ignobly destroyed.*

᠎᠎᠎

8

From the street he looked like a comet streaking across the night skies. Red and blue flames seared the heavens as Johnny Storm headed up to Westchester for his date.

Up here in the sky, ablaze as the Human Torch, he felt free and at home. Nothing could stop him now; not even the sky was his limit.

He arced over the tall buildings of the East Bronx and saw the people far below, pointing up at him in shock and disbelief. *Look up, down there,* he wanted to shout out. *I'm the Human Torch! THE HUMAN TORCH!*

Let's give 'em a show, he thought. A show only the Human Torch could create.

From his flaming fingertips came a ball of fire which shot rocket-like into the air above him, then burst into streamers of flame which cascaded downward, then evaporated before hitting the streets below. A second fireball erupted, then a third and a fourth. Now for the *coup de grâce:* with both hands wide, he circled downwards toward the ground, streams of flame licking the skies behind him. He abruptly turned and headed upward, curved at places, letting the flames streak longer behind him as he flew. In a moment he was done, and the flaming words "HAVE A GOOD DAY" lit up the night sky for miles in every direction. *That's something they won't soon forget.*

Frankie Raye's house was a white split-level with amber-colored shutters, a wide garden, and a two-car garage. Garbage cans dotted the streets; the sanitation department would be out in force tomorrow.

The Torch landed, extinguishing his flames even as his feet touched pavement. He carried an asbestos bag across his back and removed a suit Reed had sprayed with unstable molecules. Even bunched up as it had been, it wouldn't show a crease. He'd be able to knock on Frankie's door tailored as impeccably as if he had arrived there in a limousine rather than flying comet-like through the skies.

Frankie and Johnny were lovers. The song danced through his head as Frankie Raye opened the door. She wore a paisley dress with short sleeves which were bordered with white lace, and off-green shoes which matched her purse. A green ribbon was tied through her blonde hair, and her straight white teeth flashed an irresistible smile. "You're right on time, Johnny." Her voice was warm, soft. "Where's your car?"

Johnny bit his lip. "It's in the garage, Frankie. I was hoping we could use yours. Or, better yet, how about staying in? I'll order us food to be delivered."

The smile faded from the girl's face. "You flew here as the Torch?" She waited for Johnny to nod yes. "Johnny, you know . . . you've got to know how I feel about that. I—I dated you months before I learned who you were. I really like you, Johnny, perhaps more than I've ever liked anyone else. But, God . . . I can't take your being a super-hero.

58

I hate it when you're called away in the middle of a dinner to fight some ridiculous crime the police should be taking care of in the first place.

"Why do you do it, Johnny? Why can't you be normal, a real person, like everyone else? Why, Johnny? Why?"

She paced the living room before sitting on the plump white couch. Johnny wasn't sure how to reply. "I didn't ask to become what I am, Frankie. You know that as well as I do. It was an accident, a cosmic joke that I've become the butt of."

He saw Frankie was on the verge of tears. He wanted to hold her in his arms, to make her worries go away. Why did she fear him? What was there about Johnny Storm that made her cringe every time she thought of his being the Human Torch?

He sat beside her, took her arms, and held them with his hands. "Frankie, I love you. I've told you that before. I think you're wrong, though. Yes, maybe I risk my life, but there are others who do that with less assurance of surviving than I do. Policemen take risks every day. Firemen march into blazes that could consume them at any moment. None of them have any special powers, yet they still go out and risk their lives day after day.

"Damn it, Frankie. Tell me what's bothering you. Don't hold it in. I have to know if this relationship is going to grow and get better. You've got to tell me what is coming between us. What's driving us apart?"

Tears rolled down her beautiful face and she took some Kleenex from her pocketbook to wipe them dry. She got up and walked into the kitchen where she took a pitcher of cold water from the refrigerator and poured some into a glass. "It's everything, Johnny. You're risking your life, you being who you are: a hero, the center of attention. It's all that, and it isn't that, and it's a lot I can't possibly explain, and maybe something I don't even understand myself."

She paused as she drank the water in a long, continuous gulp. Then she turned from the kitchen and saw Johnny standing in the doorway. "Maybe some people aren't cut out to date super-heroes? Maybe I'm one of those people. And maybe, Johnny, maybe it's best if we don't see each other—at least not for a while. Do you understand?"

"Frankly, no, I don't. Either you care about me, or you don't. Either you love me with or without my faults, or you don't." He stepped toward the outside door and put his hand on the knob. "I don't understand you, Frankie. I thought we had something going between us."

He opened the door and walked into the cold, fresh night. The wind blew his blond hair wild. Frankie Raye stood in the doorway and watched him. "I guess I was wrong about you, Frankie. Damned shame, too. I really loved you."

Without stripping off his suit, he yelled out *"FLAME ON!"* His body suddenly ignited and he took to the skies, once more a comet streaking heavenward. Frankie Raye watched until he disappeared from view, then closed the door behind her and slowly walked to the couch. She fell on it and cried, long into the night.

"I love you, too, Johnny. Damn, I love you, and I can't ever be yours, because I'm scared . . . because I don't want a hero in my life, because I want a normal home with normal children, a normal life, and you just don't fit in, Johnny Storm.

"You're something special, and you can never be normal. You can never walk among people without having them stare at you. Even when you're not the Human Torch, even when you're Johnny Storm, you're special.

"Oh, God, Johnny, I want you so much it hurts. I want you, but I can't have you. I . . . I just can't."

Blast. Damn and double damn! What's wrong with me? Why can't I hold on to anybody? What am I doing wrong? Will somebody please tell me? Those were Johnny Storm's thoughts as he flew southward over the Bronx toward Manhattan.

Reed has Sue; even Ben, monster that he is, he has Alicia. And what've I got? Nothing. Myself! Zero! Zilch! I lost Dorrie Evans. I lost Crystal. I've lost every girl I've ever loved. Now, Frankie. Blast!

His flame shimmered red and blue as it cut a swath across the skies. He felt alone, impotent, miserable. He was twenty years old, a member of the Fantastic Four, the premier super-hero organization of its kind. He had traveled throughout the world and to other worlds. There was little he had never seen, less he had never done, yet the blond-haired youth was not satisfied.

He was alone in a world where two was the most important number. Couples. Pairs. Man and woman. Husband and wife. And he was a *one . . . a damned one.*

It wasn't his super powers that separated him from everyone else. Reed and Sue had powers certainly equal to his own. They found love and marriage and happiness together. He knew there were other heroes: Spider-Man, Iron Man, Captain America. Surely they didn't suffer as he did. They couldn't be as alone as he was.

His sister raised him as a child; she watched him grow. He was bright, though teachers had always said he never applied himself as he should.

61

He went to college, then dropped out after his first year. What could they teach him? He had been everywhere, he thought, or perhaps he rationalized.

He was good with machines. He could take apart a car and reassemble it better than it had originally been. There was nothing about motors he didn't know. He had talent, he was handsome, he was a hero.

So why couldn't he get a girl? Why didn't women return the love he felt? Why was he always alone?

His mind buzzed with questions and felt helpless when no answers became clear. What good was being a super-hero if his life was all screwed up?

He streaked across the skies, heading toward the Baxter Building. *Maybe Frankie wasn't feeling well. I'll give her a call tomorrow.*

When the belt radio buzzed and Reed Richards's voice spoke, he didn't know he wouldn't speak to Frankie Raye tomorrow. He didn't know he might never speak to Frankie Raye again.

He didn't know that by tomorrow night, there was a very good chance he would be dead.

9

Johnny landed before the double doors to the Baxter Building and saw O'Hoolihan react instantly. The heavyset doorman opened the door and bowed. "Top o' the eve, Mr. S. I sure do hope ye be feelin' good."

Johnny grinned. "Not as well as I'd like to, O'Hoolihan, but I'll make it through the night, I guess."

Inside the massive lobby, people hurriedly rushed in all directions. Johnny Storm moved away from the flow heading toward the elevators and stood in front of a single door set aside from all the others. His hand touched his belt, and an invisible light flashed from the buckle, striking a metal plate to the side of the door.

Instantly, the door slid open to reveal a private elevator. Johnny entered and pressed the bottom-most button. The first floor that housed the headquarters of the Fantastic Four contained their bedrooms, dining room, visitors' reception area, kitchen facilities, and day-to-day living space. These were all kept separate from the other four floors, which housed the F. F.'s intricate science labs, vehicle hangars, and observatory.

All five floors, the tower of the Baxter Building,

were owned by the Fantastic Four and paid for by the money Reed Richards earned from the patents on his incredible inventions.

He entered his private bedroom, removed his clothes, and took a shower. Perhaps, he thought, it was time to move out. Get his own apartment. After all, Reed and Sue had their own place, though they spent most of their time in the Baxter Building and still had bedroom facilities there, along with a second room for Franklin.

And Ben had another apartment across town, a three-room bachelor pad he could call his own. Only Johnny Storm lived full-time in their sky-scraper headquarters. *Yeah, perhaps it's time to move on.*

He stepped out of the shower and ignited him-self. His flames could dry him off faster than any towel. Within moments he was dry and dressed for action. Reed had said he wanted to speak to Johnny about something that had come up. He told him to be ready for travel if he agreed to come with them.

He sauntered down the hall and knocked on their bedroom door. Inside, he could hear the shower running as Reed opened the door, his hair still wet. "Come on in, Johnny. Sue will be right out. We've got a problem."

Johnny was interested. "Lay it on me, leader-man. What's up?"

It took less than a minute to explain the situa-tion, and Johnny listened quietly, attentively. At long last he let loose with a long whistle. "Whew! Dr. Doom. Doesn't sound good, Reed. Any idea what he's up to?"

Reed shook his head. "None. That's what bothers me. I know Doom too well. Yet he's given his promise to the others. He guaranteed their safety, that nothing would happen to them, and that he'd have them all back by Sunday night. I know this sounds strange, Johnny. But Doom doesn't lie. He's too proud, too sure of himself. If he says the people will not be harmed, despite all his evil, despite everything he has ever done to us in the past, I know he's telling the truth.

"But the problem is, I also know he would never do anything unless he means to gain something by it. I just can't analyze this situation. I can't figure out what he wants."

Johnny arched his brow. "Maybe he's telling the truth when he says he's changed his ways. Maybe he's reforming? It's happened before."

"What's happened before?" They turned to see Sue dressed in her bright blue action garb, her long blonde hair flowing free to her shoulders. "You said it happened before. What?"

"Johnny thinks Doom may have changed his spots. But like the proverbial leopard, I doubt it. No, he's up to something, and frankly, I think it's best that we go along to figure out just what it may be."

Sue combed out her hair as she spoke. "I agree with Reed, Johnny. You had to be there to understand, but Doom hasn't changed—not one whit. I sensed he relished it when Ben attacked him. I think he may have provoked the fight."

Johnny laughed. "I can see it now. My blue-eyed buddy winding up and letting go with a one-two punch, and there goes Doom's head. It must've freaked out that poor orange slob.

"I just wish I could've been there. I wouldn't've stopped laughing till tomorrow."

"Oh, I think you woulda stopped, junior . . . When I laid one o' my knuckle sandwiches on ya." Ben Grimm stood behind Johnny. " 'Sides, you woulda done the same, unless you let that robot punch you out."

Johnny spun, ready for a verbal battle. "Yeah? Listen, big shot, at least I can tell the difference between a man and a robot. Then, again, looking the way you do, I'm surprised you didn't start a fight with the cappucino machine. You know how nasty those little buggers can look."

Ben thrust his head closer to Johnny's face. "Says you, matchstick. All yer good fer is settin' off fire extinguishers. Or don't ya remember what happened at that movie ya went ta last week? Ya almost caused a panic."

Johnny pushed even closer to Ben, their noses virtually touching. "I wouldn't talk if I were you, Quasimodo. One look and half the folks ran out of the picture before it began. And they were playing *The Monster That Ate Trenton!*"

Reed's voice broke the string of verbal abuse. "That's enough out of the both of you. I asked you here, Johnny, to find out if you'll come with us. I won't force you. I know you may have other things on your mind, but—"

Johnny interrupted. "Reed, we're a team, aren't we? When we were first formed, we agreed to stay together through thick and thin, and, face it, if I could put up with Ben's ugly face peering over the morning paper before he's had his first mug of coffee, I guess I can stand trekking over to Latveria to make sure Doc Doom is on the up and up. I'm going with you, Reed. There's nothing else to say, right?"

Sue spoke first. "That's better. We've got a job to do and we do it. Doom said his jets will be taking off in the morning, that we're supposed to meet him at Kennedy Airport. I think it may be safer to get a good night's sleep now. That way we'll be ready if anything out of the ordinary does happen. Any disagreements? Ben?"

"Don't look at me, Susie. I'm the sweet one o' the group."

"I agree, Sis. I'll see you in the morning. G'night, Reed. You, too, gruesome"

"Aw, shuddup. I'm too tired ta think of a comeback."

"That must explain you all the time. You're always so tired you never think."

Johnny leaped from the room and ran down the corridor screaming. Ben Grimm was close on his tail, hurling a pillow at the fleeing figure.

Sue turned to Reed and rested her head on his shoulder. "What do you think, Reed? You've been unusually quiet."

Reed grimaced before talking, and when he did, his words were slow, deliberate. "I think we may be in for trouble. I think whatever it is Doom has prepared is so diabolical, he isn't even worried that we, his greatest foes, will be right beside him all the time.

"I think we've got to watch him very carefully, and what's more, I think we're going to have to be prepared . . . for anything!

"Sue, i won't be coming to bed tonight. I've got to go up to the lab and do some work. I'll sleep on the plane tomorrow."

Sue's face mirrored her worry. "It's that bad, Reed? Are you certain?"

Reed answered quietly. "With Doom you can't be certain about anything. But I know one thing, Sue. If I don't take the time to plan something tonight, we may not live beyond tomorrow."

Sue shuddered as Reed left their bedroom, heading to his electronics lab two floors above. It wasn't like him to be so pensive. He must have some idea as to what was going to happen to them. He has to know. And he has to be very, very worried.

She removed her costume and slipped into her night clothing. She threw off the bedspread and used only a thin sheet. The lights were turned off and Sue closed her eyes.

But it was many hours before sleep would come.

10

鸡舞舞舞舞舞舞舞舞舞舞舞舞舞舞舞舞舞舞舞舞舞舞舞舞舞舞舞舞

To anyone who looked, Latveria was a "picture-postcard" kingdom. A great golden castle sat proudly atop a high mountain peak. Small clusters of gaily colored wooden homes dotted the mountainside. Each small home had a pocket-sized garden for growing fruits and vegetables. At the base of the mountain there were several open-air markets where fresh produce and meats were sold.

There were no museums, no theaters, no sports arenas, and no churches, the latter being the only oddity that separated Latveria from the other vest-pocket countries that existed throughout southern Europe.

The humble Latverians were mostly farmers, tilling the great farm that bordered the golden castle. Wheat, corn, and barley were its principal products. Fifty percent of their gains were turned over to the castle's lord; the other fifty percent they could sell in the marketplace.

To all intents, Latveria was just another nation, neither doing particularly well, nor starving, either. The people seemed contented, though they rarely smiled, the lot of the hard-working farmer, perhaps.

Those men over the age of twenty who were

not working the farms were conscripted into the Latverian Army, where they would serve no less than a five-year term. At one other point in their lives, every Latverian male would serve at least four years. Their country was a small one; it could be gobbled up by any of the major powers at any time, or so their monarch had told them.

In truth, however, Latveria was better armed than any other European nation, as well armed as both the United States and the Soviet Union. Hidden within the mountain were missile launching sites. The great golden dome that perched atop the castle housed a massive laser cannon which could be controlled by satellites orbiting far above the Earth.

Patrolling the border were strange, silent guards. They were an army of grim, unforgiving, merciless robots who, when given a command, could turn a human body to pulp in less time than an ordinary man could eliminate a crawling ant.

The Monarch of Latveria was Dr. Doom, the cold tyrant who would brook no revolt, permit no freedoms, encourage no hopes. Yet, the Latverians, save a few rebels whom Doom would quickly eliminate as soon as their existence was discovered, didn't hate Doom. Surprisingly few ever thought of revolution. After all, their standards of living had sharply risen once Doom took power. They now had food enough for their family, freedom enough for their paltry needs, and unless they raised their voices in protest, Doom left them pretty much alone. What more could these people want? Their last ruler gave them none of Doom's benefits, and had kept their lives in constant fear.

Keep in line, be humble, do not complain. Things could be worse. These were the key words for a long life in Latveria, and most of the nation zealously observed those rules without complaint.

Old Boris greeted Doom at the small airfield to the south of the castle. "All is in readiness, sire. Living quarters have been provided for your guests." Doom nodded, pleased to see the old one.

"You are well, Boris? The medicines I left for you have cured your cold?"

"Yes, sire, they have. I no longer ache. I thank you, sire."

"Good." Doom turned toward the men and women scrambling out of the massive jets. "This is my homeland. It will be totally open for your pleasure. Feel free to go anywhere. Ask my people whatever you wish. You will learn that Doom is benevolent to his subjects. But, first, you may wish to freshen up. Follow me to the castle."

Several of the older men groaned as they saw the castle high above them. *God, do we have to walk up there?* But Doom stepped onto a slick, rubbery roadway and indicated for his guests to do the same. "We have many conveniences here in Latveria, some of which even you Americans have never seen. Observe!"

Doom touched a ring on his metallic glove, and a light flashed from the gemmed surface, striking a steel plate that was half-buried alongside the road. The rubbery surface vibrated for a moment, then began to move. "This is a mobile road. Within minutes it will whisk us up to my castle, without any expenditure of energy to you. Man was meant to spend his time in thought and contemplation, not in the needless waste of energy."

Reed Richards was impressed but kept silent. An incredible people-mover, but the work force it took to build this must have been equally incredible. And for what? The people here were not permitted to leave the country. Doom had probably forced them to build this extravagance for his own private use.

As if sensing Reed's thought, Doom spoke again. "It may interest you to know that my robot constructs built this roadway for me. My people are too valuable to have me waste their time. I do not demand their service to me, though I am their official Monarch."

The crowd was buzzing with surprise. They had always heard Doom was a despot, that his reign in Latveria was tyrannical. Could all the news reports have been wrong?

The mobile road took them into the center of town, where vendors paused in their duties to salute their Monarch. "Welcome, sire. It is good to have you home again."

A woman with a small child approached Von Doom. "Sire, I beg you to help me, to aid my son. His leg was crippled when our cart overturned. I—I cannot afford a doctor. Is there anything you can do for him, sire?"

The road slowed to a halt and Doom stepped off it. He lifted a heavy metal arm and placed it on the child's chest. "Surely you know all medical treatments are free to the poor. Take him to my castle; demand to see my private physician. He will make your son whole once again. Doom promises that."

The woman bowed and kissed Doom's hand. Tears welled in her eyes. "Oh, thank you, sire. You are as good and kind as I have always heard. I will never forget this, sire. Thank you."

The roadway moved on again, and the Americans saw Doom differently now from the way they had before. Perhaps he wore his frightening armor, but he seemed to be more of a man than they had

72

ever suspected. He seemed to care for his people. What else mattered?

As they turned out of sight, the woman saw one of Doom's personal guards approach. "Did I do well? I did as you demanded." She was frightened as the guard raised his hand and struck her swiftly across the face.

"Silence, you stupid female. Now return to your hovel. We will release your husband from prison. Be happy Doom has granted you your wish. If you did not cooperate fully, your husband would now be dead. Go, and never speak of this to anyone. Do you understand?"

The frightened woman nodded and said nothing about her crippled son. *I have been given my life,* she thought. *I dare not ask for anything more.*

To anyone who looked, Latveria was a "picture-postcard" kingdom. The people seemed contented, though they rarely smiled.

There was a reason why.

11

"This is my laboratory." Doom gestured with great pride at the massive stone room lined on all four sides with complex computers, workbenches, strangely shaped devices, vials, chemicals, papers, instruments created for purposes few men could even guess, mechanized workers hunched over ion-powered microscopes, and assorted other creations.

"In the past year alone, I have perfected wonders that will revolutionize mankind . . . fertilizers that will grow crops five times their normal size. With my wonder serums, I will eliminate hunger and disease. Give me five years and I will cure cancer. Ten more and heart attacks will be something of the past."

Reed Richards examined a strange circular device sitting on a worktable. "I've never seen anything like this before, Doom. It seems to be an element converter for transmutation, but—"

"Excellent, Richards. I see you were able to analyze my device properly. You are right, of course. I am experimenting in elementary transmutation. So far success has been limited." Doom paused, as if an idea had struck him. "If you wish to join in my research, Richards, I am sure the equations I

75

have been unable to work out will soon be answered. Are you interested?"

Reed smiled. "I'm sorry, Doom, but my research is taking me in other directions. I can't afford to take time away from my own discoveries."

"Of course, I understand, Richards. So be it. A shame, though. You and I are the two most brilliant minds this world has ever known. To work together would be an assurance of success. I understand you have your . . . pride, however." Doom paused before continuing. "Let us move on, if you don't mind. However, you may feel free to linger. My laboratory and my notes are open to you."

Ben grumbled. "I don't like this, Stretcho. He's playin' ya fer the fool. What's 'is game?"

"I wish I knew, Ben. I've never seen Doom like this. He's open, polite, courteous beyond expectation. Unless he's actually changed, he must be supremely confident in himself. There's no other explanation."

"Frankly, Reed, I'm not at all interested in this stuff. You think Doom'll mind if I scoot around town as the Torch? See if anything's going on? Maybe I'll find a girl." Johnny was bored; he wanted to move on.

"Reed, I have an idea," Sue said. "If Doom's willing to show us his castle, then whatever he has planned can't be here. What if I became invisible and scouted around some? Check things out in a way that wouldn't anger him."

Reed nodded. "Good thought. Just be careful, Sue. Stay alert. I know something's dreadfully wrong, and I don't want you to fall into any of his traps."

Sue grinned as she whispered. "How can he set a trap for an Invisible Girl? Besides, if anything happens, I have my energy powers. And I won't forget my belt radio.

"Face it, Reed, I can handle myself, even if I am just a girl, eh?"

Reed grimaced in reply. "All right, so I'm the last of the chauvinist pigs. I can't help myself, honey. I don't want anything to happen to you."

Sue bent over to kiss him on the cheek. "Worry about yourself, brown-eyes. I'm not exactly a sitting duck."

Sue's eyes closed as she concentrated, and a moment later her body faded from view. "I'll be back as soon as I can, Reed." Her voice faded as she left the room.

"Don't worry it, Stretch, Susie can handle herself. She's got powers that make us look like Howdy Doody."

Reed knew Ben was right, but he still didn't like it. True, Sue could turn herself invisible, or turn anything else invisible if she wished to—although when she did, she couldn't use her powers on herself. Sue also possessed the ability of forming energy shields, and through practice she learned to shape the energy powers into convenient forms. She could focus her powers with pinpoint precision, or spread them wide enough to shield them all.

There was little Sue Richards was incapable of doing; she had mastered her powers long ago, yet she was Reed's wife, the woman he loved more than anyone else. If she was hurt in battle, if she were to die, it would be his fault. Because of him she had been given her abilities, and he felt responsible for whatever happened to her now.

Sue quietly approached a sealed door and analyzed the lock. It was bolted from within, but it wouldn't be hard to pick, not if she could slip her force field through the controls and slide the trip-lock to the right.

No one was around; no one would see her. She'd have only a few moments before someone might come strutting down the corridor. She had to work quickly. Materializing, she concentrated her energy powers at the lock. An invisible beam of pure force snaked through the delicate instrument. Then a faint click was heard. She'd done it.

Smiling, she faded from view again and opened the door, shutting it quickly behind her. She was safe, but she'd best remain invisible. With Dr. Doom, you could never be too sure.

The room seemed to be empty: no furniture, no lights. Nothing. Yet, why was it bolted?

Quietly, she rapped on the wall closest to her. Solid. She tapped the second wall across from her. The same. But the third wall echoed with a dull thumping sound. Hollow. A secret panel?

Delicate fingers spread across the wall. If there was a secret door somewhere, she'd find it.

Her hand touched the molding that bordered the room at waist level. One small section slipped as she brushed by it, and the wall seemed to suddenly shudder.

A black line appeared at one corner. The wall was opening inward at that point. Holding her breath, she ran toward the black space. She entered the opening, and waited for her eyes to become accustomed to the darkness.

Staircase leading to where? She reached out and grabbed a narrow metal railing. *Nice of Doom to think of this,* she thought. *Easier to climb these steps in the darkness.*

The wall slid back into place as she reached the bottom of the stairwell and stepped onto a stone floor. *Must be spring-controlled. When my weight left the staircase, it closed.*

There was complete darkness here, and she used her hands to probe the way. The stone corridor was chilly, damp. She could smell the musk and it nauseated her. *This could really be nothing. Old castles always have secret corridors.*

There was a squeal behind her, and, somewhat frightened, she whirled around. Something small and hairy brushed past her. *Lord, it must've been a rat. Oh, God.*

It took a moment for her breath to return. *I may be torturing myself here for no reason.* She felt the breeze come from her right. *Must be a tunnel.* She turned and saw a faint glimmer of light ahead of her. *Well, can't turn back now. C'mon, Sue, let's go on.*

She reached a large cavern with a small table in the center. A candle resting in a cup sat on the table. A chair tucked neatly between the table legs seemed a good place to rest, if only for a moment. *Someone was here, just a few moments ago. There's no melted wax in the cup.*

She called out, "Anyone here?" No answer. Her eyes adjusted to the faint glow and she could see the corridor she had come through. It continued on past the cavern on the other side. *Whoever it was had to go that way.* She scratched her neck, pushed the hair out of her eyes, and stood up again. *May as well go on.*

Suddenly there was the scraping sound of steel. A heavy door slid down from the roof of the cavern and sealed off one of the tunnels. She turned toward the other. It was still open. She ran toward it, fear beginning to take hold of her. A second steel door descended.

A bolt of energy shot out from Sue's temples as

she rushed forward. It formed a cushion between the floor and the lowering door. The door jammed into the force cushion with a loud crackling noise. It held. *Have to expand the shield. Force open the door. This is a trap. I've got to warn the others.*

She felt herself grow heavy, tired. Her eyes searched out the candle on the table. *Oh, my God . . . of course. It's burning a sleep gas. That candle was set there to stop me.*

Instinctively, she threw a force globe around the candle, and the buffer beneath the door faded from view. The door slammed down, and the echo of steel against stone seemed like sarcastic laughter.

Her hands groped for her belt radio. *Damn it, static. I'm too far underground. Either that or Doom had this tunnel especially created to prevent radio waves from piercing it.*

She was breathing hard now. *What do I do? Invisibility won't help here. If I remove my force shield from the candle, the gas will put me to sleep. My powers are useless.*

She felt utterly defeated and sank to the chair. *Reed warned me, but like a proud fool, I didn't listen.*

Then, from the ceiling, she saw the glint of steel. Small openings appeared in the rock. Five tiny openings that began to glow red.

A thin beam of light streamed from one opening. It flashed across the chasm and bounced off the floor, ricocheted off the stone wall, and continued its zig-zag pattern. A second beam from a second opening followed it. Then a third, a fourth, and finally the fifth.

Lasers!

Heaven help me, lasers everywhere— Sue dived off the chair a moment before a ruby beam splintered it. Instantly, the chair disintegrated. A second beam hit the table and bounced off. *It must be coated with something.* She saw the candle still lit atop it. *Of course, Doom doesn't want the candle snuffed out.*

The beams criss-crossed the room in a random, helter-skelter pattern. One of them would strike her at any moment—unless she surrounded herself in a force field.

An invisible ball of energy formed about her as a laser blast struck the shield and skidded off into the wall. *Safe, but for how long? I can't keep the shield in place for more than fifteen minutes. Then what?*

Sue Richards had a reason to worry. She had a quarter of an hour to effect an escape, or she would be sliced to so many ribbons.

What do I do? What the hell do I do?

12

Johnny Storm yawned as he circled the Latverian village. *Borrrring!* He had come with the others, hoping to get into action. He wanted to do something, anything, to forget about Frankie Raye. But he couldn't shove her beautiful face from his thoughts. She haunted him every moment. Wherever he looked, he saw her.

Below him, he could see the Latverian farmers staring up in horror. Was he a demon? One of Doom's treacherous devices come to spy on them? They turned from their flaming visitor and returned to their work. If he was with Doom, he would see them working hard. That would please their iron-clad master.

What I need, Johnny concluded, *is to find someone my own age. Not everyone here is old. Or are they?*

He flew lower over the small huts and saw a teen-ager tending a small private garden. The boy felt the heat on his back and turned to see Johnny Storm standing behind him. "Who are you?" He stared at Johnny questioningly. Latveria was a small country. No one was permitted entrance; no one was allowed to leave. Soon you learned who everyone was. This blond stranger was not one of them.

"Who are you?" he repeated. "How did you get in here? The gate was locked."

Johnny flashed a smile. "My name's Johnny Storm. From America. I was, uh, brought here by your leader." The boy stared at Johnny. Then his eyes grew narrow.

"Go away. Leave me alone. I do my work. I do not want to be bothered." He turned and ignored the stranger. If he came here with Doom, he belonged to Doom. It was best not to consort with Doom's men. You could die that way.

But Johnny was persistent. "C'mon. I'm not with Dr. Doom. You don't have to fear me."

The youth turned again and studied Johnny. He was not like Doom's men. He had an easy smile; his eyes showed no signs of evil. Perhaps he had been too hasty.

"I am Erich."

Johnny extended a hand, but when Erich failed to take it, he let it drop to his side. "Erich, you wouldn't happen to know where I could find any girls around here. My age?"

The Latverian youth smiled. His fears vanished. With a nod, he bid Johnny to follow him.

Doom continued: ". . . and this is my royal chamber. The bed has been created especially for me. The linens are sewn here in Latveria by my handmaidens. The women among you will appreciate the finely spun cloth and the expertise of the seamstresses. Please, all of you, as you return home accept from me a sample of their work. I insist on it."

Reed hung back, Ben at his side. "All appears to be normal, Ben. Too normal."

The Thing nodded in agreement. "Hey, Susie ain't come back yet. Ya think somethin' happened?"

Reed suppressed a grimace. "Let me try to raise her on the belt radio." His fingers fumbled with the switch as he moved from one frequency to the next. He clenched his teeth as worry overtook him. "She's not answering, Ben. I don't like this. None of this."

Ben was ready to move. "That tears it, Stretch. I'm gonna squeeze that tin-can's neck till he talks."

"No, Ben. Doom won't miss us if we split off from the crowd. Let's check this out first. If we don't find Sue, then we'll confront him . . . and we'll do it away from the others. I don't want anyone hurt." He saw Ben was grumbling The big man would love to tear Doom apart for any number of reasons. "Do you understand that, Ben?"

Ben hissed his answer. "I understand it, Mister. I just don't have ta like it. That crumbbum an' me go together like salt an' a wound. Whenever I see 'im, I just wanna clobber 'im but good."

"If we don't find Sue, you'll get your chance. I promise you that. Now, come on, we've got work to do."

They ran through the corridor to where Sue had left them. Reed glanced down the hallway and said, "She could've taken either of those doors. We'll split up. First one to find her, contact the other—immediately. And that means no fighting, Ben. I want the three of us together before we decide what to do."

"Sure, sure. No scrappin'. I gotcha, Reed." *'Course, if I just happen ta knock a few heads together 'fore I give ya the signal, what the heck, right?*

The door Ben opened took him into a wide courtyard made of stone. Suits of armor stood in the wide archways. Long spears were at their sides. At the far end of the court, there were two mounted knights on stone horses.

Above him was a wide balcony, and a carved stone fence ran the whole distance around it. Directly over him a crystal chandelier hung in place.

To his back was the door he had just entered, and across the courtyard was the door he headed for.

"Blasted place looks like a blamed museum. How can that tin-plated tyrant *live* here? Ya can't put yer feet up on a table when the blamed table's prob'ly worth more'n you are."

He heard a creaking sound come from behind him. He whirled in time to see a steel door slide in front of the wooden door he had come through. Another steel door slid in front of the door at the far end of the courtyard.

"So, we wuz right, Doom, wuzn't we? Yer playin' games with us? Well, yer crazy if ya think a little piece o' tin's gonna stop the ever-lovin', blue-eyed Thing."

Ben lumbered toward the far door. No use going back. As he reached the center of the court, he heard the squeak of steel grinding against steel. Out of the corner of his eye, he saw what was making the sound.

"Kiss my fanny. It ain't possible." The suit of armor closest to him creaked off its pedestal, its lance in its hand. "I ain't asleep, and this certainly ain't no knightmare."

Stiffly, the armored form plodded toward the orange behemoth, its limbs moving more smoothly with every step it took. A second suit of armor leaped off its pedestal and lifted its lance for an attack.

86

Ben saw three more such suits move and approach him, slowly at first, but as each became more accustomed to movement, it speeded up, stepped more naturally.

"Awright, ya bozos!" Ben shouted at no one in particular. "Lemme see what yer made of."

With astonishing speed, he grabbed the first suit. His powerful fingers closed vise-like on its arm. Silently, the living armament thrust its lance into Ben's stomach. The steel crackled with raw energy. One thousand painful volts of electricity jolted their way through the Thing's massive hand.

Instinctively, he fell back and dropped to the floor, grabbing his burning hand with his other. "Blasted thing's hot-wired. Now what'll I do?"

Ben heard the footstep behind him and he whirled as two lances smashed into him. His rocky hide sizzled and he yelped in pain.

Scrambling, he made his way to the far end of the courtyard. His deep blue eyes grew wide and horrified; ten suits of armor marched toward him, their lances ready for attack, their expressionless faces seeming to leer in ghoulish delight.

They paused and turned their armored heads toward the two corners of the room. At once, the two massive suits poised atop their stone steeds came to life. The horses reared, their legs clawed the air, and then they leaped from their pedestals and galloped toward the Thing.

That was the signal to begin.

They moved in.

And Ben felt the stone wall press against his back.

The door Reed Richards opened revealed a large, seemingly endless series of corridors that crisscrossed each other, came to abrupt dead ends, led back to their starting point, and proved to be nothing less than an intricate maze.

Reed stretched above the maze and saw at the far end an open door beyond which was a one-way mirror. Through the mirror Reed could see Sue. She darted in terror from flashing red lights that appeared for a moment, then vanished, only to reappear from another direction. He saw a beam flash across Sue's forehead. She grabbed her head painfully. Blood oozed through her gloved fingertips.

"Don't worry, Sue, I'll help you. I swear I will." Reed was frantic. Those lights were undoubtedly lasers. Doom was attacking her, but nothing could keep Reed from reaching his wife's side.

Instantly, the ceiling buzzed with an electronic hum. Reed saw it lowering. He ducked back into his corridor and the ceiling came to rest atop the maze walls.

This was a game, then. A test. Doom had allowed Reed to see his wife facing almost imminent death. Reed would be anxious now, frightened for his wife's safety—mad, perhaps to the point of throwing all caution to the wind. He wanted Reed's veneer of scientific logic stripped away. He wanted Reed Richards dead, but he wanted him to die crawling like the peasant Doom thought him to be.

Reed Richards the scientist was now a trapped rat in a maze. His wife's safety was his incentive to reach the end of the maze.

And now, to add some impetus to his efforts.

A gurgling sound like water rushing through pipes came from behind Reed. He saw a small grating in the wall of the maze about ten feet up from ground level. Then the water came gushing out.

Only it wasn't water. Reed recognized the heavy

overpowering stench, and it flowed slowly, viscously.

There was no doubt about it.

The liquid that came gushing toward him was —*sulfuric acid!*

He stretched instantly toward the far end of the corridor and followed its turn to the left. Three corridors branched off before him. He remembered seeing them from above. One turned back upon itself. A second was a dead end. The third continued to another corridor and another and another. But, which was which?

Then the maze was plunged into darkness.

13

༺༺༺༺༺༺༺༺༺༺༺༺༺༺༺༺༺༺༺༺༺༺༺༺༺༺༺༺༺

"John Storm, this is Anna. Anna, John has come from America." Erich smiled at the raven-haired girl, slightly younger than Johnny. She was beautiful in her long lilac dress with the puffed shoulders and lace at the end of the flared sleeves.

Johnny stood back and took a long appreciative look. The girl was absolutely lovely, her face flawless; she wore no makeup, nor did she need any. Her green eyes sparkled delightfully; her lips were soft and moist. Johnny thought of Frankie Raye and her Bloomingdale's pantsuits, expensive makeup, and Vidal Sassoon hair-styling, then stared at this peasant girl in her simple homemade dress, her naturally long hair, which draped her soft, milk-white shoulders, and the unpretentious, unhurried aura she seemed to radiate.

Anna, in her natural simplicity, was a more lovely, vivacious woman than Frankie had ever been. Johnny grinned, like a fool, he thought, and extended his hand to Anna. "I'm very pleased to meet you, Anna. *Very* pleased." He stammered and Anna blushed.

She bowed timidly. "I have heard of you. You are one of the Fantastic Four, no?" Her voice was as soft and warm as her small, fragile hand. "You once battled with our Monarch?"

Johnny nodded, unsure what to say. Would she defend Doom? Was she against the metal-clad tyrant? All at once he remembered he was no longer in America, where freedom was taken for granted. He was in Latveria, where strangers were looked at askance, where there was hardly a voice raised against the mad Monarch, who ruled everyone with an iron hand.

He saw the hurt in her eyes. She was young, but she had felt the cruel hand of tragedy in her life. "That is good. Doom is a despot. I would see him dead before my own eyes are shut forever."

The intensity of her hatred startled him. What could Doom have done to her? he wondered. Did he dare lay his hand upon her? Johnny cringed at the thought, and it made his blood boil with rage.

Erich saw the mood overcome her, and saw the confusion in Johnny's eyes. "She was betrothed once, my friend—to one of the rebels in the underground. Doom's robot army found them and destroyed them all. It was horrible. For days their bodies were displayed in the public square as a reminder of what Doom would do to any who dared plot against him."

Johnny's voice was soft. "I—I didn't know. I'm sorry, Anna. I truly am. If there was anything I could have done . . ." He stopped. There was nothing. It was already over with.

Anna forced a weak smile. "I am pleased you are here because you may be our people's only hope. We suffer every day, John Storm. We are thought of as cattle to be herded about as Doom's mad army demands. We fear for our lives; we rarely voice our discontent. To do so may mean

92

death or worse. Doom is capable of inflicting terrifying torture."

Johnny looked confused. "I—my friends and I
—came through town. People bowed to Doom
reverently; they seemed joyful in their admiration.
He's brought prosperity to Latveria, raised your
standard of living. I—don't think me wrong if I
say this, Anna, but I don't understand. What has
Doom done to hurt your people?"

Anna looked hurt. "He has given us food and
has taken away our freedom. When Doom first
took over Latveria, we were a joyous people. Then
he created his robot army, his terrible machines,
his network of spies. Many, if not most, of our
people decided resistance was futile. They gave
themselves to Doom, sold themselves into slavery
for a morsel of food.

"They worship Doom because they fear him, not
because they have love for the iron Monarch. They
trained themselves to think Doom cares for them.
Today they believe it. But there are a few who
know that Doom is evil; they plot against his reign
of terror. One day, they hope, they will be strong
enough to fight him and, if God is on their side, to
destroy him.

"John Storm, will you join with them? You and
your friends have powers that could stop Doom.
You are the only ones he fears. I—they—are sure
you could beat him and return Latveria to its people. Will you help us?"

He gazed into her eyes and saw them fill with
tears. They pleaded with him. Her soft hands took
his and held them with promise.

His fingers pulled at the flesh on his face. He
didn't know how to answer. Read would never
allow them to join in a battle against Doom. Doom
broke no international law; he attacked no other

nation. He may be a despot and a mad dictator, but there were many others, and the Fantastic Four didn't traipse into their countries and wrest away control.

They were among the most powerful human beings on Earth, but their power didn't give them the right to remove governments they disagreed with. Not even the United Nations had that awesome power.

He wanted to help. His every gut reaction was to say yes, but sadly he shook his head. "I can't. You don't understand, but my friends and I just can't do that."

Her voice sharpened. "You condone what Doom has done?"

"No. I hate Doom. I've fought him a dozen times before. I would like to see him done away with for the good of everyone. But I can't help you. My friends can't help. We just can't fight every dictator who—"

"You can help, but you won't." Her voice was filled with venom. "I thought you were different from the others. I thought you were heroes. Instead, you are like all the others. You talk about loving peace, but you do nothing to achieve it. Good-bye, John Storm."

She turned and stalked off, Erich was quiet, and Johnny stood silent, dumbfounded. It hurt him to see that lovely face so filled with anger and hatred.

He began to call after her but stopped himself. He stared for a moment at Erich, but said nothing.

"*FLAME ON!*" he shouted, and his body instantly ignited. He streaked through the sky back toward the castle.

He wanted to see Reed immediately. He needed advice.

14

He hadn't heard them flying up behind him until the first missile streaked past him. He dived and arced back. Three interceptor jets were on his tail, even as a second set of missiles was launched at him.

Johnny Storm flew downward, and the missiles instantly changed their course. *Heat seekers.* He strained to speed up, to fly faster. He had to evade the missiles, no matter what.

Doom was attacking him. That meant he had probably done the same with the others. They may have been captured or killed by now. He flew in a tight circle and sent a concentrated blast of heat toward the first of the three missiles. It made contact and the explosion knocked him back for a moment.

Two missiles closed in on him as he arced upward toward the jets. The missiles were on his tail, closing in now. He was incapable of increasing his speed. He couldn't spare the time to fire another blast at them. He'd get one, but the final missile would surely find its target.

Abruptly, he dived again as a plan was formulated. He watched the missiles spin. There was a several-seconds delay between his actions and theirs. Good enough.

He formed a wide circle and saw the missiles closing the gap between them. It would only be a matter of seconds now.

Straining with all his power, he streaked toward the jet closest to him. The missiles closed in. They were less than thirty feet behind him. In ten seconds they would hit and he'd be blown out of the sky. He pushed on, strained as he had never strained before. He had to pull ahead, just briefly, just for a moment.

The jet was directly above him now, the missiles directly below. Inside the fighter, the pilot saw a blue-red bolt of flame heading directly toward his fuselage. For a moment he panicked; then he remembered—Doom had outfitted the jets with a new flame-resistant asbestos.

Johnny was mere feet from the fighter. Then, suddenly, he arced up and back, flying as far as he possibly could. The missiles began their turn. But they were a moment too slow.

The jet incinerated on contact, destroyed by the very missile it had fired.

Two more jets pursued the Human Torch. They had seen what Johnny had done. They wouldn't fire their heat seekers until they had him dead in their sights.

Bullets exploded from their mounted guns. Johnny heard them rushing toward him and he extended his heat field. It would slow him down a bit, but the wide heat pattern would melt the deadly lead long before it could hit him.

How to get rid of two fighter jets was the only thought running through the Human Torch's mind. Deliberately, he flew up and wide, circling the jets and coming down behind them. He fired a concentrated heat blast at them. The jets were sprayed with fire, but they rocketed on undisturbed. Doom had obviously protected them. He expected a battle. Everything to date had been planned.

But what did Doom want? Why did he lure the Fantastic Four to his kingdom? What was he after? Johnny didn't know, and at that moment he didn't much care.

Leaving a long stream of flame behind him, Johnny headed toward the mountains. If he kept low and flew between the peaks, he'd lose the fighters. They weren't as agile as he, couldn't maneuver as well, and certainly couldn't land as quickly.

Determined to evade the fighters, Johnny pressed on. The high peaks were several miles off. He could make it and then rest a bit. His flame wouldn't stay ignited for much longer, not with all the energy he'd expended. He'd flame out in ten minutes and would then have to rest almost half an hour to be at peak capacity again. If he could survive that long.

The mountains were topped with snow. That wouldn't help him. The cold would make it take that much longer for him to be able to flame on again. But he had no choice. His time was running out.

He flew low over the peaks and cut between two jutting rocks. One jet veered off; the other stayed on his trail. Johnny landed for a moment, caught his breath, then flamed on again. *They aren't going to leave me alone, are they?*

There was a deep canyon on the other side of the twin peaks. He dived low. The jet followed him and fired a volley of bullets at its flaming target. If only one got through the burning red glow that surrounded the Human Torch, that would be enough.

Suddenly, Johnny turned right and came up behind the fighter. He matched the jet's speed and caught onto its tail. It took all his strength to resist the winds which mercilessly battered him. He had to hold on, just a few minutes more.

The twin turbos were directly to his side. The jet may be flameproof, but if he could get in one good shot at the turbos, that would be all he needed.

The jet jerked to the left, and Johnny was almost thrown from it. His hands grabbed the tail wing and he held fast. He braced his back against the wing and with all his power he aimed one full heat blast into the left turbo.

Instantly, he flew up and off as the plane exploded in a massive purple and black cloud of smoke.

Johnny tumbled back from the impact and he saw the final jet circle toward him. He was dead, he told himself. No way to survive this one. His flame was almost exhausted. He had only enough power to land and keep himself warm. There was nothing he could do to attack.

He let his flame fizzle out and he fell groundward. Conserve all his energy, free-fall until the last moment, then flame on again and land safely. It was his only hope. If he could hide himself in the caves, he might make it. Unless the cold killed him first.

He tumbled downward, spread his arms and legs wide, as would a parachutist. He began to glide along the wind currents; he felt the cold breeze invigorate him. He felt alive and fresh and momentarily distracted. Up here he was a different man; nothing could bother him. Nothing could disturb him.

The ground seemed to take its time moving up to meet him. The expanse of whiteness made it difficult to judge distances, but Johnny didn't care. He would float and float until there were only feet left to fall.

The bitter wind stung his face, and cold froze his open mouth. His eyes began to water and tear, the world became blurry, and all he could hear was his body rushing headlong toward the ground.

How much longer before flaming on? he wondered. He couldn't see through the tears, he couldn't make any judgment, yet the thrill of freefall still clung to him.

Then there was softness and he was no longer falling. He hadn't flamed on. He hadn't landed. Where was he? With his hands he cleared the water from his eyes. There was whiteness everywhere he looked. Reality gripped him; then terror overtook reality.

Where was he?

His arms jutted out and felt a plastic softness all around him. He was encased in something, but what?

He tried to flame on, but found he couldn't. There was some sort of gas in here, something that made it impossible to use his power.

What the hell was going on? *What?*

He felt tired, his eyes smarted from the gas, his head became thick and cloudy. He struggled to keep open his eyes but found them closing against his will.

He jerked back and forth, trying to rip through the softness that held him prisoner, but he was unable to lift his arms. They fell heavily to his sides as his legs crumpled under him.

He fell to his knees as his eyes shut totally.

And in a moment he was asleep, quiet as a babe, and just as helpless.

The pilot glanced at the monitor to his side. The camera mounted beneath the jet fighter showed part of the cable that hung from the bomb-bay door and the white plastic bubble that was attached to the cable. He could imagine his prisoner asleep inside the bubble.

Dr. Doom had been right. The fool would waste his power battling two fighters, but the third would hang back until he was tired and weak. And then they would have their fourth and final prisoner.

The pilot pressed a button next to the monitor.

Doom paused before the great iron door. Behind him, the Americans waited anxiously. This had been a tour they would long remember. "My friends, I am about to show you my collection of art. No Westerner has ever before seen its magnificence. I do hope you find it as pleasing as do I."

His iron glove glanced over the electric eye and the door creaked open. Doom stood on the side as his visitors entered. He could hear them gasping with delight. What beauty! What wonders!

Above the door a red light flickered for a moment. No one but Doom saw the faint glow. Beneath his great mask Doom allowed himself a rare smile.

The last of the Fantastic Four was now his captive. And soon, they would all be dead.

Doom entered the expansive gallery and watched the American fools moving from one painting to the next, their eyes wide in appreciation. This was all booty the Nazis had stolen during World War II. Treasures Doom had stolen from them in turn.

There were Rembrandts, Goyas, Cézannes, Michelangelos, Da Vincis, Monets, Manets, Picassos, and dozens more. His collection was worth in the tens of millions, and it genuinely pleased him that the Americans appreciated its value.

Tomorrow he would return the Americans to New York. For years they would talk about their journey here, how magnanimous Doom had been, how wonderful was his great castle, how much the people of Latveria loved their Monarch. The time and expense were worth it, Doom felt. *Let the world believe I am a merciful ruler. It will only buy me time.*

The time I need to garner the power I must have, if I am to accomplish my true objective.

No one heard the soft, sinister chuckle that echoed through the gallery.

15

᠎ᡌᡌ

The Americans waited for the buses that would take them to the airport. The room was buzzing with excitement. Their trip had been everything Doom had promised and even more. They would have stories to tell their children and their grandchildren. Latveria may be a small country, but it was virtually a paradise.

Dean Collins felt humbled by everything he saw. Doom had used his genius to help his people. His castle was a veritable museum, a treasure-house of art. Perhaps, he wondered, had he been wrong about Doom all along? The man had been conceited once, but he was much younger then. Perhaps he had outgrown his earlier attitudes. After all, his deeds seemed to prove he had.

He glanced around, then saw Doom standing in the doorway. "Where are Reed Richards and the others?" he asked, worried.

Doom nodded. "My friends have decided to stay here a while longer. Dr. Richards wished to work in my laboratory. He decided to work with me on some personal projects."

Collins was suspicious. That didn't sound like Reed, not the Reed Richards he knew. "I'd like to

103

say good-bye to him, if you don't mind." Something was wrong, Collins felt.

Doom bowed. "Dr. Richards asked not to be disturbed; however, I am sure he will not mind if you speak to him." His hand pressed a button beneath a television screen. "This should buzz in the laboratory."

The TV screen flicked on. Reed Richards's face appeared. He smiled. "What is it?"

Doom gestured toward Collins. "Move closer to the screen. Otherwise, the camera cannot pick you up." Collins moved in and felt relieved. Reed seemed to be all right.

"I wanted to say good-bye, Reed. Doom said you were lagging behind?"

Reed smiled. "His laboratory fascinates me, Dean Collins. He has several devices here that I've never seen before. I can't leave yet, not until he shows me how they're used. Ben, Sue, and Johnny are staying here with me. By the way, how'd you and Mrs. Collins enjoy the tour?"

Collins returned Reed's smile. "We loved it. I'd stay behind myself if I could. But duty calls. Tomorrow I've got to be back on the golf green. Ah, retirement."

"Enjoy your trip, Dean Collins. I've got to go. Good-bye." The television screen flickered for a moment, then went gray.

Dean Collins turned to the others and said, "All right, what are we waiting for?" He put his arm around his wife and led her toward the first of the buses.

He hummed. He had misjudged Doom. A tiger can change its stripes.

Doom wrung his heavy iron-bound hands in satisfaction. The contemptible fool had bought it all.

In another room of the castle, technicians removed the Reed Richards rubber face mask from the faceless robot programmed to mimic Reed's voice and mannerisms. It had functioned as perfectly as designed. But then, Dr. Doom had built the robot, and Doom never failed.

16

ᘓᘔᘓᘔᘓᘔᘓᘔᘓᘔᘓᘔᘓᘔᘓᘔᘓᘔᘓᘔᘓᘔᘓᘔᘓᘔᘓᘔᘓᘔᘓᘔᘓᘔᘓᘔ

"Are you leaving now, sire?" Boris asked. The old man was seated in a chair next to Doom's throne. Doom activated four viewscreens mounted to the wall of his private chambers. On the first he saw Johnny Storm, still unconscious, in a specially designed room which would prevent the youngster from using his accursed flame. When Storm revived, he would have a surprise in store for him.

The second screen revealed Sue Richards crouched in a corner of the catacomb, the lasers cutting a destructive path in every direction. Her energy powers would soon fade, and she would either be cut down by the death rays, or by the fumes from the poisonous candle.

Reed Richards's plight was more amusing. He rushed blindly through the darkened maze, a torrent of acid about to engulf him at any moment. It would not be long before Doom's longtime foe was little more than a burned-up cinder.

The final screen revealed Ben Grimm battling one of Doom's robot knights. The monstrous Thing grabbed an electrified lance and tossed it aside, his hands burning with pain. The mounted knights chased him across the long courtyard. He wouldn't escape. He couldn't. Even if Grimm defeated his robots, as unlikely as that might seem, there were dozens more. Each one he destroyed would be instantly replaced. They would never tire, but already Grimm's massive hands rose slower than they had before. His punches were less effective than they had previously been.

Doom flicked off the screens. His foes would be dead very soon. No need to linger. "Yes, I will be leaving, Boris," he answered finally. "Is my private jet prepared for my trip to America?"

His old servant nodded slowly. "It is, sire. All is in readiness."

Doom rose and left the room, and Boris hobbled after him. Doom was surely after something terrible, Boris thought. His actions these past several days had been carefully planned for months. But what was it Doom wanted? Not even his faithful servant Boris knew the answer. Doom wouldn't reveal his plan, only that he was going to America, and that what he wanted was somewhere in the Baxter Building—the headquarters of the Fantastic Four.

And that is why he spent millions in luring the fabled foursome to his country under the guise of a tour for his old classmates. That is why he spent millions more preparing very special traps designed to capture and destroy his old foes.

But what Doom's final objective was, only Doom knew.

Boris glanced at the calendar on the wall. Doom had said he wanted success on Walpurgis night— his birthday. That was tomorrow night.

Whatever it was Doom had planned would occur tomorrow, May 1.

Boris shuddered in horror. He intimately knew the details of Doom's origin. He was able to guess at Doom's secret. If it was what Boris suspected, even the heavens would roar in horror.

Doom turned toward his old friend. "You will look after the castle for me, Boris? Only you can I trust."

Boris bowed reverently. "I will look after everything, sire. To serve you is my only desire."

Doom left and Boris waited until the dull thud of metal boots striking stone steps finally faded. Then, when he could no longer hear anything save the crickets, he closed his eyes and fervently prayed.

〰〰〰〰〰〰〰〰〰〰〰〰〰〰〰〰〰〰〰〰〰〰〰〰〰

17

Doom entered his private jet and sat in a wide plush chair. He pressed a button on the control board at his side. The robot pilot was activated; the jet would now take off and he would be in America by dawn.

Tomorrow was his birthday, and all had been planned for the special gift he had promised himself. He closed his eyes as the jet shuddered to life. He would sleep now and awaken upon landing. He needed all his strength.

He dreamed. He first saw soft clouds and bright blue sky. He saw rainbows long and beautiful. He saw himself as a boy sitting at a campfire, his handsome father at his side. His father had a broad smile as he sang a ribald song. Other Gypsies laughed in response. He saw his father's medicine bag at his side. It was always at his side in case it was needed. His father had been a great, caring man.

Then the smile faded from his father's face as he stood up and bade Victor to follow him. The young boy did as his father commanded.

They walked through the forest to the edge of their small village. He listened as his father spoke. "Someday, Victor," he had said, "you will be the last Von Doom. You must always remember your heritage, my son. Always remember your father loved you, that we come from a proud line of Gypsies." Young Victor said nothing, but he listened intently.

At the edge of the forest there was a small cemetery. The markers were crude stones carved with chisel and hammer. They stood before one stone that simply said "Cynthia Von Doom." Victor realized why he had been brought here. Today was his birthday, May 1. Every May they came to this cemetery to honor his mother.

"Your mother loved you, Victor, as much as I do. She wanted her only son to be a big, tall, handsome man—one great in pride and strength. She wanted her only son to be a good man, compassionate, merciful, loving."

His father paused and held Victor with both hands as he stared into the young boy's eyes. "Do you understand that, my son? Strength and compassion, pride and humility. They go hand in hand. Without one, the other is abused. Without compassion to temper strength, there is only the basest of bullies. Without humility to temper pride, there is only arrogance. Do you understand that, Victor? It is important that you do."

Victor said yes. He understood, although he thought his father was wrong. Mother was compassionate, and the Baron's men abused her. She had great humility, and the Baron's men embarrassed her, slaughtered her like an animal. What good were compassion and humility to his mother? They served to have her slain by wanton cowards.

No, strength was important. It could put down those who would seek to humble me. Pride was important. It permitted others to know whom they could not push about.

112

But Doom simply nodded in answer to his father's question. He was such a good man that he failed to see how important strength and pride could be. He loved his father and did not want to argue with him. Saying yes would please his father, and that is all he wanted to do just then. Later, when he was older, he would show his father the errors of his ways.

They bowed before the gravestone and said a prayer. Werner Von Doom shuddered a bit. It was no use, he knew. His son didn't hear or didn't believe a word he had said. He could see the bitterness set deep in Victor's eyes. *My Lord,* Werner thought, *so young, and so much like his dear mother.*

He feard his son, feared this child's intensity and ability to hate. Cynthia was as intense, but she didn't hate. That was the difference. She could be loving, giving. She used her witchly powers for good, not bad. She used her spells to help fertilize their gardens, to help heal their sick, to protect them from attack. But in Victor, he sensed only the power, not the compassion. The world would one day hear about this boy. Victor would grow into manhood with terrifying powers—powers that would lead to his own destruction . . . or the destruction of his pursuers.

All this Werner saw in Victor's deepset, brooding eyes. He grasped his son's hand and the young boy looked up at his father. "Yes, Father? What is it?"

Werner smiled weakly. "Nothing, Victor. Let us go home. We still have to make our dinner, eh?" Right now the boy was young. But soon . . . much too soon . . .

Doom's eyes opened as the jet began its descent. The airport had been notified that Doom the First

113

was arriving. New York's mayor offered a diplomatic ceremony, but the Latverian embassy said Doom preferred a simple limousine, which they would prepare for their Monarch.

He disembarked and climbed into the car. The next stop was the embassy, and from there, the Baxter Building.

18

Doom waved his hand across the electric eye, and the elevator door instantly slid open. It had been simplicity itself to duplicate the exact code necessary to open the private elevator of the Fantastic Four.

What would come next would not be simple. Doom braced himself as the elevator reached the proper floor. He was unable to learn how to properly enter his foe's central headquarters. There would be an arsenal of weapons waiting to attack him. He breathed in deeply. Now he was ready.

The door opened to an outer lobby. Before him were two more doors. Solid steel. They would have to be blasted.

He raised his hand and a bolt of white light flashed from his fingers, bathing the doors in an eerie, unearthly glow. The door convulsed, creaked, shimmered, then dissolved into a slag of molten metal.

From inside there came a faint clicking sound. Doom was alerted. The protection devices had snapped on.

Beyond the door Doom could see the visitors' reception room. There wouldn't be any traps there. Too many uninitiated cretins waited in this outer lobby until one of the Fantastic Four would come to greet them. No, Richards wouldn't allow them to come to accidental harm. The dolt was concerned with human lives; he would do nothing to endanger any man. And that is why Richards and his foolish friends would die and Doom would win. After all, nothing would come between Doom and complete victory.

With an arrogant gesture, he blasted the reception area door from its hinges and stepped inside. Daniel in the lion's den, he thought. If his hideous mask could smile, it would.

From the floor came a sudden grinding noise. He had stepped on a large square, one of many, yet this one vibrated ever so slightly. He could discern a slight separation between this tile and the one that bordered it. All this he noticed in a fraction of a second, even as a square of plexiglass shot up from the slight separation and attached itself to the ceiling. Doom was surrounded in a plexiglass prison.

"You are a fool, Reed Richards. To think this paltry prison could long stop Victor Von Doom!" He extended his iron arm and grasped the side of the plexiglass with his fingers. "I have no need to even use my incredible powers."

His fingers pressed outward with incredible force. His iron armor was an exo-skeleton which increased his strength a hundredfold and more. The glass cracked into a spider-web design. Then Doom smashed the prison into a thousand flying fragments with the back of his heavy glove.

"I know you, Richards!" Doom shouted, fully aware his foe was more than five thousand miles away, if he weren't already dead by now. "You wouldn't create devices to harm a man. Your weaponry is designed to capture, to imprison, to disarm.

You are too weak to kill a fool who deserves death. That shall be your undoing."

Doom knew the plans to the Baxter Building. The thirty-fourth floor housed the Fantastic Four's living quarters. There were kitchen facilities, dining rooms, bathrooms, and four bedrooms. The thirty-fifth floor contained their recreation rooms, gymnasium, meditation chamber, and monitoring rooms. The thirty-sixth floor contained all of Reed Richards's labs. Anything he had to build could be constructed there.

What Doom wanted was on the thirty-seventh floor. Above him, on the top of the Fantastic Four's five-floor headquarters, were the vehicle maintenance shops, the hangars, and the entrance to the retractable rooftop observatory. Along the side of the headquarters was their rocket silo.

Suddenly, Doom sensed gas spreading through the hallway. Instantly the oxygen system built into his armor was activated. All airholes were covered with a thin, transparent glass.

He made his way to the elevators. These responded to a different code from the ones in the lobby. He placed his fingers along the control panel, then his armor's computers whirled into frenzied activity. "Damn." Doom was angry. They could only be activated by the special fingerprint patterns programmed into Richards's computer.

He had to get upstairs. His fingers clawed the control panel a second time. A white gas spread from them. As the gas touched the metal plate, it became solid, icy. Freezing white ice spread over the panel and the elevator door, covering it completely. Doom stepped back. With every second the ice would get colder until it finally reached absolute zero. But the door would crack long before then.

Within moments the door crumbled to the ground, a useless pile of icy shards. Ignoring them, Doom entered the elevator. His fingers pressed the automatic button. The elevator would rise now.

The elevator rumbled, then ground to a sudden halt. A voice filtered over the sound system. It was Reed Richards, and it took Doom a moment to realize the voice had been taped and programmed.

"To whomever has entered the private elevator of the Fantastic Four: This is Reed Richards. You are trespassing on our property. If you have made it this far, undoubtedly you have encountered several other devices. But I warn you now, you will not penetrate our inner headquarters. I have constructed a series of elaborate protective weapons that will guarantee the sanctity of our headquarters. To go farther would be to risk your life. This has been a warning. I suggest you press the button marked 'Exit.' The elevator will take you to a side corridor where you will find a stairwell allowing you to leave unharmed.

"Remember, you have been warned. We are no longer responsible for what may next happen. Consider your alternatives." The tape clicked off.

Without pausing, Doom again pressed the button marked "thirty-seven," then dashed off the elevator. The car dropped suddenly out of view. No matter which button was pressed, the car would head for the corridor Richards had mentioned and deposit the trespasser by the staircase.

"You are clever, Richards. Too clever for your own good. But soon you shall meet defeat at the hands of Dr. Doom."

The elevator shaft was empty now. Doom peered upward and stared into the darkness. *This is the only way. I have no other choice.*

His powerful hands gripped the heavy steel

118

cables. One hand reached above the other, pulling him upward. There was little problem climbing this way, even with the incredible weight of his armor, but it annoyed Doom to have to use physical force. That was beneath him. He was pleased Richards would soon die, if he already hadn't been burned to a final cinder.

Gas spread through the tunnel, but the mask's glass filters were still in place. Angrily, Doom continued his climb.

From the walls, lasers snapped into view. Beams criss-crossed in all directions, bouncing off Doom's armor. Long ago he had coated his armor with an anti-laser refracting base. Once more Richards had been checkmated.

He paused for a moment; his feet searched out a small ledge. "Damn you, Richards. Damn you for this inconvenience." Never before had Doom had to work so. With his powers, he always took what he wanted.

As he passed the elevator door on the thirty-fifth floor, the sonic bombardment began. It cut through his armor the way a sharpened scythe slashed through a field of wheat. His head reeled back painfully, his eyes closed into thin slits, and tears poured from them.

The sharp sound rumbled through his brain, his body was in agony, his arms twitched, his legs flailed helplessly. He felt his fingers loosening their grip on the cable. He forced himself to stare downward. If he fell, there would be a thirty-five-story drop. Not even he would survive.

His fingers struggled to maintain balance as he fought to control his mind. He had to shake off the pain the sonics created. He had to close his mind to everything but his mission.

Quietly, he recited ancient prayers forgotten

119

long before the days of the Druids. His mind reached outward and inward; he thought of his mission, his mother, his childhood, his face, his awful, disgusting face. How handsome he had once been, how proud he had been of his manly features. And now, what was it? A scarred, disfigured, pulpy mass of twisted flesh and scabbed sores.

He remembered his mother's diary, the curses, the visions, the oaths. He had never mastered sorcery the way his mother had. Science was his to command. He could create whatever he needed. But sorcery eluded him. He wanted that knowledge, knew it was his birthright. He had to possess complete knowledge of the Dark Arts; otherwise, his destiny could never be fulfilled.

He wanted power, the power to destroy all his enemies, the power to rule a world, the power to rule the universe itself. But to do so he needed control over the evil ones, the dark forces, the creatures of hell. He needed to blend his mysticism with his science. No one could defeat him then. No man would dare try.

He heard his breath hissing through his mask; he heard his metal feet clanging against the steellined corridor. Then he realized the sonic blast which attacked him had abated. It was over.

Quickly, without pause, he climbed the cables. He thought of nothing but reaching the thirty-seventh floor. Hand over hand, his feet hooked the cables and pushed him upward. It was only a matter of moments now. He could see the elevator door above him, a shining beacon indicating freedom. It drew closer, became larger. Then, at last, it was beside him. He blasted the door off its hinges and he leaped to safety.

He made it. He had conquered death once more.

Invigorated with renewed pride, he shouted to the world at the top of his voice, "I am victorious! I have won! I am Victor Von Doom. Let the world beware my awesome power!"

And now, he thought, he need only find what he had come here for.

"Soon, very soon, the Negative Zone will be mine!"

19

Reed Richards was running for his life. He heard the sulfuric acid roaring along behind him. The corridor came to an end. *What do I do now?* he asked himself. *I've got to remember the pattern.* He had seen the intricate maze for only a moment before the ceiling forced him downward, but a moment was all he needed. His photographic memory would do the rest.

If he had time to think, which he hadn't. And if he could see the maze, which he couldn't. He stretched his hands out as far as they could go. One hand took the right tunnel, the other the left. The left met resistance fifty feet up. He ran toward the right.

The acid gushed toward him, filling up the left-hand chamber and flowing through the right. If he had taken the wrong turn, he would be dead at this moment.

He kept the fear from gnawing at him. Just concentrate. Think before you take any step. Sort out all the confusion and just plunge on.

The tunnel continued, but there was another tunnel branching off to the left. He stretched his hands out again. The left tunnel branched into two more tunnels. There was no way to know if they continued on or met dead ends. The right tunnel circled a bit, then veered sharply to the left. Reed couldn't stretch his hand any farther. And he was unable to remember the twisted route. Whatever he did, it had to be by instinct.

Two tunnels to the left, one straight ahead. How would Doom construct the maze? He heard the acid gushing toward him, slapping against the corridor walls. The right tunnel circled around. All three tunnels were longer than Reed could stretch. He made a decision.

He headed toward the corridor on the right. With all his speed he ran, his hands feeling the path before him. Doom would round one tunnel to make it seem it was coming back on itself. But Reed, in his anxiety, was able to stretch farther than Doom had expected. He had felt the tunnel veer sharply toward the door at the far end of the maze. This had to be the correct way. If he were wrong, he wouldn't suffer long.

His pulse rate increased; he felt his heart pounding. Reed Richards was not a young man any longer. Perhaps Johnny could keep running at top speed, but Reed would soon slow down, and the acid would soon engulf him.

Reed thought of his son Franklin, born just five years before. He might never seen him again.

Once more the tunnel branched off into two. The right corridor was blocked fifty feet up. He had to take the left. Reed ran, puffing, his heart tripping. Pain cut through his lungs. He found it hard to breathe. But he continued. Step after step after step.

Then he remembered. He turned back and ran toward the righthand cutoff. He could see the maze clearly in his mind. Halfway down the corridor he felt a small opening on the left. He had seen it when he had stretched over the maze. The tunnel opening was two feet off the ground, and a hole only one foot wide. He hadn't felt it when he checked this tunnel because his hand stretched toward the end, down the center. It didn't snake along the sides.

Like a snake, he slithered though the hole and found another corridor. He paused for a moment. It would take a few minutes for the acid to fill the tunnel he had just run through. A few minutes before it would reach the hole and seep on through.

He desperately needed those few minutes to calm his heart, to slow down his hurried breathing. At last he heard the wave of acid crash down the tunnel behind him. He had to begin running again.

Three more tunnels appeared before him. One, he knew would lead to the exit door. The other two would bring him closer to death. The corridors were too long to stretch forth his arms. Once more a decision had to be made. Which corridor? Which?

No way to decide. He anchored his legs at the wall and stretched down the left corridor as swiftly as he could. It circled to the right, then the left. It cut back on itself. Reed snapped his elongated body back to the starting point.

The wave of acid crashed down the corridor. He didn't have time to try testing the next tunnel. He had to make his decision. He ran down the center tunnel. He veered first to the right, then the left.

Then, for the first time, his face contorted in horror.

Before him was a blank wall. He had made the wrong decision.

Sue Richards felt her force shield fading. It could last only a few moments longer. The laser

125

beams flashed by her, picked up speed, richocheted off walls. They glanced off her force bubble, arced up toward the ceiling, bounced back and skidded off the table.

"The table?" Sue was astonished. "How in the world did I miss the obvious?"

She ran toward the table and ducked under it. She allowed her force shield to fade, and slipped a smaller one over the candle. She could maintain control over that force bubble with ease.

A laser ray hit the wall and flashed toward her. She fell back and pulled the table on its side. The ray hit it and glanced off. Doom had made the table impervious to lasers. Sue could use it as a shield.

She backed herself into a corner. *Can't let a ray hit me from behind.*

In the center of the room she saw the candle on the floor, still burning within the bubble of energy. "Got to snuff that damned thing out. Don't want to waste any energy."

The force bubble contracted. It slipped under the wick and cut it. The flame sputtered for a moment, then died out. Sue breathed easier. "Now what do I do?" she asked, uncertain.

For a few minutes she rested, the overturned table reflecting dozens of laser blasts. "Could try to blast my way out of here with a massive force bolt at the door, but if it's not strong enough, I'll be trapped. I couldn't budge the door when I tried earlier, but then—" She remembered. The candle had made her drowsy. It's possible that she was unable to use her full power.

But she was still weak. It still seemed so hopeless.

She saw Franklin playing in the field outside their country home. He was such a bright boy, so eager, so filled with joy. She wanted to be with him now, she wanted to hug him, to smother him with a mother's kisses.

Agatha Harkness came into view. The tall, thin, gray-haired old woman with the craggy features and harsh eyes was actually a warm, loving housekeeper. She saw Franklin running toward the cliffs. How many times had Sue warned him away from there? He ran; then he tripped and he fell.

Below him, Sue could see a long mountainside and a river flowing past its base; rocks lined the river. Franklin's body would be dashed on those rocks. He'd die.

Then she saw Agatha standing by the cliff. She waved her hands above her head, and twin bolts appeared which flared out and formed a circle of light around Franklin's falling body. The boy hovered for a moment in the lights; then he rose in the air, and the light brought him to safety. He came to rest in Agatha's scrawny arms.

Sue winced. She should've been there. She should have stayed with her child. It was her duty. Why did she abandon Franklin to run around the world? How could she show him the love he needed? She should be at her son's side.

But how could she be? She had been given these powers. They made her different. Long ago, when the four of them learned how the cosmic rays had affected them, they had sworn to use their powers to benefit mankind. To not use them would be to waste them.

They had been given abilities that made them more than human, but to use them properly meant they had to make certain sacrifices others were never called upon to make.

More than human and less than human. That's what they were, and that knowledge bothered Sue.

She wanted to be with her son, but she was unable to abandon her duty.

Yet, Franklin was happy. He was astonishingly intelligent, ready to help, willing to do anything. He read voraciously; his imagination was limitless. Perhaps Sue hadn't failed him. When they were together, they had a more intense relationship than any other family. They could pack more into those hours and days than other families could accomplish in weeks.

Was it the time one spent, or the quality? Sue didn't know, but she understood that the question demanded answers. When they returned home. *If* they returned home.

She felt her powers increasing again. She was almost at full capacity. Just a few minutes more . . . all she had to do was hold on tight. A few minutes . . . that's all.

The time dragged on inexorably. Sue's forehead was slick with sweat. She bit her lip waiting. She wondered what had happened to Reed and the others. Was Johnny all right? Did Doom get Ben?

Not knowing hurt her more than she could realize. The Fantastic Four was a family unit. They lived together. They battled together. If one of them died, what would happen to the others?

She fought to control her breathing, to calm herself down. Behind the table she would be safe.

Now she was ready. Sue steadied herself, pressed her back firmly to the wall to brace herself. She would have to use every ounce of willpower she could possibly muster. She would have to use her energy powers as she never had before. She counted backwards from *ten* . . . *nine* . . . *eight* . . . *seven* . . . Sue felt her veins tighten, her body grow tense. *Six* . . . Her head pounded. *Five* . . . *four* . . . *three* . . . What would happen if she failed? she wondered. Would there be time for a second chance? No way. One try. Blow out the door. Run. Find the others. *Two* . . . She prayed. She had never been religious, but she prayed now. *ONE!*

She fell back against the wall, her eyes wide, unfocused. An almost invisible ball of pure energy grew from her temple. It moved slowly at first in the direction of the door. It grew larger, it picked up speed, larger, faster, larger, larger, larger . . . faster, faster—

IMPACT!

A moment of silence, then the door shuddered and creaked and groaned, then blew apart into so many atoms. The wall now held a gaping hole.

Sue was momentarily dazed. It took several seconds for her eyes to focus, to realize where she was, what she had just done. She felt the blood drain from her. She was weak, yet she forced herself to stand, lifting the table above her, and she ran.

Toward the gaping hole she ran as if her life depended on it.

She ran *because* her life *did* depend on it.

She dived through the hole and sat in the long corridor, and was terribly, terribly weak. And then she allowed herself to cry.

"Awright, ya two-bit tin yahoos. Ya may not have known it before, but right now it's CLOB-BERIN' TIME!" Ben leaped toward the horse and rider. He didn't seem to care as his body shuddered with electricity. He was the Thing. He could fight the pain.

"C'mon, baby, let's see what ya can do." He was taunting the knight, knowing it was only a machine, incapable of reacting to Ben's sarcasm, but it made the burly ex-football player feel just a bit better.

He tossed the robot knight from the horse, then threw it at the other robots slowly marching toward him. "Lemme see, strike or spare?" Two knights blew apart under the impact. There were still eight more. "Not bad. Not good, but not bad."

He leaped over one knight, his monstrous body incredibly agile. He glanced upward and grinned. "All right, ya bozos, this is where we separate the monsters from the robots. Ya ready, tin-heads?"

The second horse and rider lunged at him. The lance struck Ben's shoulder, and he collapsed in pain. "Blazes, ya think ya'd give some sorta rallyin' cry before ya struck. Ain'tcha got no manners?"

Can the jokes, gruesome. This ain't no game. They're after me. They got the power ta cut me inta little orange ribbons. Play it safe.

The Thing forced himself to stand. The horse was rearing. It would charge again. To his side, on the wall, he saw a fancy tapestry. Doom had said it was worth more than thirty thousand dollars. *Tough!*

The horse charged, and Ben ripped the tapestry from the wall. "Ya look cold, tinny. Mebbe ya better cover yerself with a blanket." He heaved the tapestry over the two, and the horse thrashed blindly. The knight ripped at the tapestry; he tried to pull it away from his sensors. But Ben was already atop him, pummeling him with his massive orange fists.

"Ya ain't gettin' outta this, creepo. There ain't nothin' the ever-lovin' blue-eyed Thing can't clobber if he's got a mind ta."

Ben saw the other knights approaching him. He'd have to leap from the horse, get to cover. But first—

130

He swung his right hand back behind him. His blue eyes glowed brightly in the dim-lit arena. His wide, brutish mouth was turned in a sneer.

Then, in a wide, powerful arc, his hand flashed forward. His fist rammed into the robot knight. There was a loud mechanical explosion, and Ben fell off the horse as the rider found himself blown into useless rubbish.

"Yer not doin' too bad, blue-eyes. Keep this up an' somebody'll probably pin a medal on ya, providin' they can find a place ta do the pinnin'."

Like a human dreadnaught, Ben smashed his way through the robots. Their lances smashed against his brickish skin, but he submerged the pain. *Ain't good for a monster ta cry. Ain't no good fer my rep.*

He felt his back explode with fire. Two knights were behind him, their lances still embedded in his rocky hide. *God, can't take the pain; it's rippin' me apart. Tearin' me up. Gotta fight it. Gotta fight it.*

Gotta pull the blasted lance outta me. Can't cry . . . there, got it. But it's burnin' up my hand. Burnin' me up real bad. Gotta hold on . . . gotta keep strugglin'. Keep on fightin'. Can't fall. Sue an' Reed an' even the kid may be in trouble. Gotta help 'em. They'll need me. Gotta help.

He staggered forward, the electrified lances still in his hand. His vision was blurred, his legs weak. He could barely think, yet there was only one thing he could do.

He fell back to the wall and saw the remaining knights marching toward him, their lances firm in their armored hands. He tilted his head upward and he said, "It ain't gonna be easy, but I don't do anythin' the easy way, do I?"

With incredible power, he heaved the burning lance. It cut through the chain high overhead. The chandelier swayed for a moment, uncertain whether to fall or not. Then it made up its mind and plunged downward atop the marching knights.

Electricity sputtered wildly; sparks flew everywhere. There was a single corruscating squeal, and then silence.

Ben fell back, breathed heavily, and just stared. "Brush my buns. It worked. I don't believe it, but it worked."

With powerful hands, he ripped the heavy steel door from its hinges and tossed it aside. *"Now ta find the others."*

20

Johnny Storm awoke with a start. "Where am I?" he inquired. There was darkness everywhere. There was no answer. Either he was alone, or the other party wasn't talking. Total silence. Johnny could hear only one man breathing. He was alone.

His head ached and he still felt tired. *I hadda be drugged. Nothing else could explain it. Drugged and brought here, wherever here is.*

He stood up and felt the walls. They were soft to his touch. Not stone, certainly. But what? *Well, no use staying in the dark,* he thought.

He tried to flame on. He concentrated, but he was unable to ignite. "What the hell's going on here? Who's doing this? C'mon, where are ya?" *Doom! It has to be Doom. He's behind all of this. He lured us here. But what do I do about it? I can't seem to flame on.*

He sat down again. *There's gotta be a way outta here.* Reed had always told him to think out his plans thoroughly before deciding on a course of action. Don't waste your power needlessly. Think. Think! THINK!

Doom has somehow canceled my powers. How? I don't feel any different. I can eliminate the internal factors. . . . He may have drugged me, but I don't think so. My vision's clear. Heartbeat's normal. Something external caused this. But what? How?

The room? Possible! Air seems normal. Don't feel any air pressure. So what did he do? With great care, Johnny Storm ran his fingers over the walls. No projections coming from anywhere. He crouched to his knees. Nothing from the baseboard.

He stood up and tried to ignite again. His finger flickered a bit, then nothing. *Something in this room has got to be affecting me. But what?*

Anguished, he wrung his hands together. They felt greasy. There was some coating on them. Johnny approached the dim light bulb. It glinted dully off a thin filmy substance that coated his hand.

"That's it. It's got to be. He's put something on me. I've got to get it off." His sharp nails scraped the palm of his hand when he heard the sound come from behind him. He whirled and saw a fan in the ceiling begin to spin. No air blew from it. Suddenly he realized; it was sucking the air up through an exhaust system. Doom was pumping the air out of the room.

"No! You can't!" Johnny shouted, fear welling in the pit of his stomach. "Don't do this to me! You can't!" No use . . . Doom wanted him to die. Screaming would only make him use up his diminishing air supply that much sooner.

He fell to the floor. *Gotta keep quiet. Rest. Stay low. Take it easy.* He breathed slowly; he remained relaxed. But he continued to scrape clean his palm.

No use, he thought. *It'll take too long to clean this garbage off me. And by the time I do, I won't be able to use my flame. There won't be any oxygen left for me to burn.*

Whatever I'm gonna do, I've gotta do it fast. In five minutes there won't be any air left. He tore off his shirt and ripped it into small rags. *They'll absorb this greasy stuff faster than my hands could scrape it away.*

With savage fervor he rubbed at his right arm and hand. He scraped away the greasy film that covered him. He concentrated; his hand flared for a moment, then faded. Not enough. *Still not enough.* He worked with a second rag, then a third. His face was sweating with anxiety.

He heard himself gulping for air. He staggered forward to the door, tripped, fell. He lifted himself to his feet again and fell forward, this time to the wall. Grabbing with his hands, he pulled himself along the wall as he felt his feet weaken from under him. He could barely stand up. Could barely walk. But he had to make it to the door.

He stumbled and turned, then tripped backward. The door was next to him now. He could feel the knob in his sweaty hand. Now, with all his concentration, with every fiber of his being behind him, he willed his hand to ignite. He would center all his power into one hand. If that wasn't enough to do the job, it would all be over.

The door itself was steel, but the frame around it was something different, something plastic. It glowed under the heat, turned bright red, then blue, then white. It began to shift form, to melt, to drip.

Johnny felt the pain overwhelm him. There was so little air to begin with, and his flame was using what was left. He had less than a minute left. He fell to his knees and felt a sharp pain stab through his legs. He had to ignore it, ignore everything but the flame. Had to keep the flame glowing, had to keep burning the framework around the door.

Suddenly, he felt a cool breeze wash across his

135

face. Johnny stared up through half-closed eyes. There was a tiny puncture in the doorframe.

The air gushed through the hole, enlarging it. Johnny grinned as the coldness whipped past him. Hungrily, he swallowed the air, let it play in his throat. Then he collapsed.

He was unconscious for only a moment. His eyes opened and he saw two vague figures before him. They sharpened into view.

"Figgers, junior. Yer always takin' a nap. Didn't ya get no sleep?" Ben Grimm's voice could not be mistaken.

"You great big ape. Get me outta here." Johnny extended a hand as Ben ripped the door off its frame. "Just tell me one thing, big fella. Where were you when I needed you?"

"Playin' games with a bunch o' King Arthur rejects."

The other figure stepped into view. "Are you all right, Johnny? What happened in there?" Sue was plainly worried. "I found Ben and then we heard you groaning."

"I guess I'm fine. Just barely. Doom tried to kill me. He almost succeeded. Hey, where's Reed?" He was sorry he had asked almost as soon as he spoke. Sue's chin was trembling; her eyes were liquid. "What happened to him? Tell me, damn it. Tell me!"

Ben shook his head and grumbled. "We don't know, kid. We ain't been able ta find 'im. We searched everywhere."

Sue's voice quivered with fear. "I'm scared, Johnny. I don't know what Doom's done to him. What if he's—" She couldn't bring herself to finish her thought.

Johnny was grim-faced. "Then we'll split up and search some more. I don't think Doom would've taken Reed away—not and keep us here. Search every corridor, check if doors lead to phony doors. Knowing Doom, it's possible Reed was right before us, only we just didn't see him. Fan out."

"You don't have to." A trembling, weak voice came from behind them. They whirled and saw Reed propped against a pillar, his costume torn, his face white. He staggered forward almost out of control. Then he fell. Ben caught him in his massive arms.

"Stretcho! Wha' happened?"

Sue pushed passed Johnny and took Reed's hand. "Darling, talk. . . . What did Doom do to you? Please, for God's sake, tell me. I've got to know."

For several agonizingly long minutes, Reed let his breath return. He waited until he could easily open his eyes. Johnny fetched him some water. Slowly, carefully, he drank it, savoring each mouthful. "I was trapped like a rat in a maze," he began. "Trapped, with nowhere to go, no lights to see by, and a torrent of burning acid crashing toward me."

He saw Sue tremble. He lowered his voice to calm her. "I had taken the wrong tunnel hoping to find the maze's exit. Somehow I had to get through the gushing torrent of acid and head for the correct corridor.

"I could hear the wave rushing toward me, but that was all I heard. I realized then that Doom had shut off the flow of acid into the maze. I also knew that the acid had by now branched off into every corridor, filling each tunnel as it passed by. I was in the farthest section of the maze, and the torrent had diminished by the time it had reached me. There was enough to flow through the tunnel, certainly enough to burn me if it hit me, but not enough to fill the tunnel from the floor to roof."

He paused again, took another sip of water. It hurt him to talk. He still felt the pains of his escape. Ben scowled. "C'mon! C'mon! This is like the end of a serial chapter. I ain't waitin' till next week ta find out how ya escaped. Talk, big man . . . talk!"

Reed smiled weakly. He saw the others relax. Ben's offhanded humor always eased any situation. The big, brawny Thing had a way of seeing right through to the humor of any given problem. "All right, all right," Reed allowed. "Just give me a moment."

He sipped some more water, then felt the strength return to his aching bones. "I stretched toward the ceiling, and propped my arms and legs against the walls. I was a paper-thin blanket slithering over the torrent. An occasional wave washed by me. I wanted to scream, to grab my wounds, but if I did, I'd drop to my death.

"I had to press on, fight the pain, edge my way to the end of the corridor, take the other tunnel and continue across the roof until I reached the door. That's where I faced my toughest problem. I had to somehow open the door without burning my hand. Unfortunately, the doorknob was under the current of acid. There was no way I could get to it.

"I stretched my hand toward my boot. That was the thickest part of my costume. I knew I had to take the risk; otherwise, I would eventually weaken and drop.

"With my hand inside my boot, I reached into the acid. The boot began to smoke instantly. You all know I constructed our costumes out of unstable molecules. It allows me to stretch inside my uniform, Johnny to flame on without destroying his, Sue to turn invisible and take her costume

138

with her. Unstable molecules can do almost any-thing, but they still burned. I felt acid trickle in, but I kept my hand inside the boot and guided it blindly toward the knob. My fingers began to burn, but I couldn't stop. I had no choice. The pain be-came terrible. I thought I would black out at any moment, but I didn't. Sometimes I wish I had. My face was contorted; I was crying from the terrible pain. It would have been much easier to give in.

"But finally, the door opened. I stretched through, stayed on the ceiling until I was far from the maze. Then, finally, I fell to the floor, where I heard voices. I was still too dazed to realize they were yours, but I inched forward, ready to fight. Then I heard Ben speak, and I knew that voice could belong to only one man. That's it. That's all."

Ben Grimm scratched his brickish chin. "Ya see, even when I ain't around, I save lives. I'm a regular Florrie Nightingale."

Johnny shot Ben a glance, then smiled. "You mean Daffy Duck, Ben. Both of you are quacks."

A huge orange arm shot out, and four stubby fingers grabbed Johnny's waist and hoisted him in the air. "Wha'd ya say, junior? Ya mind repeatin' it so's I can hear ya an' respond in a manner fittin' yer statement?"

"All right, you two, stow it. We haven't got the time for bickering." Reed stood up, shaky at first. "I want to find Doom, now!"

21

There were five guards waiting for them at the end of the corridor. Their guns were drawn, ready to fire. Ben shot a glance at Reed. "Want me ta take care of them, Stretch?" He cocked his fist in gleeful anticipation.

Reed shook his head. "I want them stopped, not crippled. Sue—?"

Sue nodded and stepped into action. Five separate energy bubbles appeared around the astonished guards. They tried to fire their guns, but the bullets wouldn't emerge from their chambers; Sue had clogged them with separate energy bursts.

Reed approached them with confidence. "Where is Doom?" They didn't know.

"I don't believe 'em, high-pockets. Gimme a chance ta work 'em over a bit."

"No, Ben. They're telling the truth. Doom wouldn't bother telling any lackeys his plans. C'mon. I want to get to his central complex."

They rushed through the corridors, Johnny flying behind them. "Reed, what makes you think Doom isn't here? You seem to think he's left."

"Our escapes wouldn't have been possible if Doom was monitoring us, Johnny. In every case he could have made some adjustment, held us back, possibly have succeeded in destroying us. I think he's left, but I don't know where he's heading, unless—" His eyes grew wide with realization.

"Blast it! Of course! Why didn't I realize it? This was all a setup to capture us—to take us away from New York. Whatever Doom is after, it's back in the States. And unless I miss my bet, it has to do with our headquarters. Doom wants something inside the Baxter Building, and to get it, he had to get us out of the way."

They entered Doom's main control room, and Reed saw Boris sitting in a wooden chair next to Doom's throne. The old man looked weak, and not at all surprised to see his master's enemies standing there, still alive.

"I am pleased you lived. Death can be so horrible," he said, his voice soft.

Ben plodded toward him. "I didn't see ya tryin' ta stop Doomsie, little man. Ya just stand right next ta him an' do everythin' that blasted walkin' can-opener tells ya ta do."

Boris let his fingertips run across his face. He was old, perhaps too old. He should have died many years ago, but his curse was continued life. "Doom is my master. I must honor him. I cannot disobey him. But you cannot understand that. You do not know me, our people, our ways. I may not approve of his actions, but long ago I swore to his father that I would remain at his son's side until I died. I have kept that promise for many, many years. I intend to fulfill that promise until I am relieved."

Reed interrupted. "Where has Doom gone to? America? The Baxter Building? Please, you've got to tell us. Many lives depend on your answer."

Boris shut his eyes and welcomed the darkness. "He has gone to claim his destiny. He has lived his entire life for this day. At this moment, his jet is nearing your homeland. Soon he will enter your headquarters. It seems, sir, that you and my master have been competing with each other for years. Both of you are brilliant men, equally brilliant, I would say. For each discovery you have made, my master has made an equally ingenious discovery. But you have succeeded in one area that has always eluded my master, from before the days of the explosion. Time after time he has met failure trying to uncover what you already had learned. At last, he felt, he could wait no more."

Johnny felt the anger overcome him. He grabbed the old man by the collar. "So he tries to kill us and take what he wants. What kind of madman do you serve? How can you accept him? Don't you have any gumption, man? How can you just sit there and serve that maniacal killer?"

"Leave him alone, Johnny. We've got what we came for. Let's go." Reed put his hand on the youngster's shoulder and urged him away. "We've got a long trip back to America."

They ran from the castle into a band of robot sentries. Laser pistols were drawn and aimed at them. Johnny took to the air, flaming on as the Human Torch. With his arms outstretched, he unleashed a volley of fireballs at his targets.

Ben Grimm leaped at one robot and squeezed its base until the mechanoid shuddered and blew apart. A second robot fired at him; the blast grazed his shoulder. Ben fell forward, tumbling behind a massive rock.

With a herculean effort, he hefted the twelve-ton boulder and hurled it at the steel assassin who had shot him. He grabbed another robot and tossed it more than half a mile away into a small stream.

Reed Richards felt the laser blast skim by him,

143

missing by a fraction of an inch. He was still weak, but these robots were not about to stop him. Not now. He stretched thin and wide and oozed beneath several robots. As the sentries adjusted their rifles, he came up around them, enveloped them. His fingers stretched toward their controls, broke open the control box, and ripped the main fuses from their housings. The robots fell dead to the ground, useless piles of metal junk.

Sue Richards faded from view and ran toward a rocky area. Three robots pursued her, their radar picking up her electronic heat pattern. Laser blasts flashed on all sides of her as she ran for shelter. They homed in on her with deadly accuracy. Instantly, she became visible again, with a force shield formed before her. Laser blasts splayed off it, then vanished.

With a massive display of power, she threw the force field toward the sentries. Like a battering ram, it knocked them off their pins, sent them scattering.

She sensed another robot approaching her from the rear. A second robot was at her side. She dived between them, they fired, but she rolled out of the way. Then she smiled briefly.

Sue paused, allowed the robots to adjust their aim. Without moving, she turned the robot behind her invisible. She had to time this correctly. If she was a fraction of a second off, she would be caught in their crossfire.

As one, they fired their lasers as she dived from sight behind a wide oak tree. She heard the invisible robot scream as its companion blasted it apart. A moment later she saw its scattered fragments littering the ground.

Reed stretched toward her, grabbed her hand,

and tossed her to Ben. Johnny Storm flew in low. "I got this one, Reed," he said, firing his concentrated heat blast at the sentry. The robot halted instantly, shimmered, then flowed to the ground as molten steel.

Johnny flew high again, then stared at the area around them. "Some more sentries headed this way, Reed." Johnny pointed north. "Let's intercept the buggers."

Reed shouted in protest. "No. We can't take the risk. Let's run the other way. Besides, we have to reach the airport. It's our only way out of here."

Johnny flew above them, scouting the area as they ran. Suddenly, he arced low and flew toward them. "Several dozen sentries are closing in on all sides, Reed. These look bigger than the ones we just fought."

"Any way out, Johnny?"

"Yeah. They've left an opening, but it takes us through the village. If they catch us there, innocent people could be caught in the fighting."

Reed grimaced. "I'm certain that was their strategy, Johnny. They're leading us on like cattle."

"Big deal. We can stay here an' clobber 'em." Ben Grimm was ready. "Or mebbe yer too chicken ta face 'em again."

Ben, Johnny, and Sue waited for Reed's reply. "We can't let them fight us here. There are too many of them, and I can't be sure we can take them on. Our only hope is to make it through the village and head directly for the airport. It may be dangerous, but it's the only choice left to us. You with me?"

Sue grabbed Reed's arm. "Of course, Reed." She stared at Ben. "Ben? Are you coming?"

Ben nodded reluctantly. "Well, I ain't got anythin' better ta do. Awright, so we paint the town red. Big deal. Hoo-hah! Let's go, awready!"

"Then, let's move," Reed said, trying to be hopeful, but failing miserably. "We make it through town, and the next stop is home."

22

As they watched the Fantastic Four running down their main avenue, Doom's robot sentries on their tail, firing their dreaded laser rifles, the frightened Latverians ran into their homes, bolted their locks, and prayed that this battle, like the ones before it, would pass them by. They had often been caught between Doom's troops and runaways. Over the years they came to realize no harm would befall them if they simply minded their own business, locked themselves away, and came out again when the church bells chimed, indicating all was once more clear.

A miniature missile exploded on the road before the Fantastic Four. "We ain't gonna make it, Stretch. Let's stand still an' fight 'em. Runnin' won't get us anythin' but killed!" Ben Grimm shouted; his voice rang like cannon fire.

Johnny Storm circled and fired at the onrushing army. A wall of fire sprang up before them, but the robots braved their way through. "I think Doom prepared these guys for us, Reed. They're fire-proof."

Reed leaped at a tree, his hands grabbing its trunk. He saw another oak across the narrow street. "Ben!" he shouted. "Grab my legs! Tie them around that other tree!"

"Huh? What're ya doin' now, big-brain? Gonna pretend yer a clothesline an' hope they'll pass us by?"

A volley of missiles was fired at them. Reed relaxed his body as he stretched into a wide sheet. The missiles hit him, three in the chest, two in the stomach. Sue shut her eyes in horror. Ben's fingers, firm on a tree stump, closed tight. The stump shattered under his grip.

The missiles stretched Reed's body backward. He seemed to elongate almost to the end of the block. Concentrating, Reed snapped his body forward like a rubber band, shooting the missiles back at Doom's robots. Four were instantly destroyed. The shattered fragments lodged in two others. All six were useless.

"C'mon, let's go!" Reed shouted, his long legs leading the four of them. He stretched upward toward Johnny, saw three divisions of robot sentries approaching from varying directions. There were just too many of them. They'd never make it out of Latveria alive.

"Come, this way, hurry. You haven't any time." It was a girl's voice that called out to them.

Reed shrank back to normal height. "Who are you?"

The girl shouted at him angrily. "There isn't time for introductions. If you want to live, follow me. Hurry."

Reed turned to the others. "There's no other choice. Let's go."

They ran down a side street and ducked through a low door. Johnny landed behind them and followed. A dark tunnel appeared before them, but the girl held a small candle which she had picked up at the door. "Follow me. Be quiet," she whispered softly.

It took several minutes, but they soon found themselves in a small wine cellar. Large casks sat on heavy wooden shelves. There was barely enough space to breathe in. But Johnny saw the girl who had led them to safety, and he gulped. "Anna? You?"

The dark-haired Latverian glared at Johnny. "Perhaps now you know what I meant when I said Doom was evil. You refused to help free Latveria, but I will still help you."

The others looked on in confusion. Johnny grinned sheepishly. Introductions and explanations were definitely in order. "I met Anna while you three were getting yourselves captured. She and I sort of had an argument." He shrugged his shoulders noncommittally.

Then Anna spoke. Her words were bitter, yet without hatred. "I wanted, I pleaded, with him to help us overthrow the despot who rules us. He refused."

Reed understood. "Johnny was right, Anna. As much as we would like to see Doom done away with, we can't enter any country we wish to just to overthrow its leaders. That would be an abuse of our powers, and, worse, that would force us to become the decision-makers between who is right and wrong, who should live and who should die. If Doom hasn't that right, we can't claim it, either."

Reed saw the girl was beginning to complain. He continued, not letting her speak. "What would happen if we, on our own, decided the government of America was unjust, or England, or the Soviet Union? We know, we can feel for those who live in oppressed nations, but we dare not use our powers to destroy their leaders. You have to fight for yourself. That's the only answer."

The girl was angry; the words sputtered from her lips. "That is the coward's decision. Doom is evil. He subjugates his people. We have no freedoms. We want to be free, and to be free we need your help. Cowards. Liars. That's what you people are."

From the distance they heard an old man's voice call out. "Anna, come up here quickly. His sentries are at the door. I want you by my side."

With a sneer on her lips, Anna mounted the steps and vanished. "Yes, Grandfather. Hold on. I will be there."

"Awright, Reed, whadda we do now? That gal thinks we're lower'n scum. She ain't gonna raise a hand ta save us, and we're trapped down here."

They eyed the large casks of wine. Reed studied them carefully.

"I have an idea," is all he said.

"Have you seen the Americans?" The robot pushed its way into the small house; its scanners analyzed the room's interior. No excessive heat patterns. "Speak!" Its voice was cold and mechanical, deliberately designed to instill fear.

"No. I haven't seen anyone," the girl said. Her eyes grew narrow, her hateful expression lost on the steel sentry.

"You lie. Perspiration rate has increased. Heartbeat has increased. You have lied. Where are the strangers? Take us to them or face immediate elimination."

The old man hobbled toward the robot sentries, his cane tapping on the wood-planked floor. "My granddaughter said she saw them earlier, when they came. Yesterday. She is not lying. Check me if you think so. I have not seen them."

"You tell the truth, yet you lie. There is something amiss. Is this your only cluster of rooms?"

There was no point in lying. The robot sensors would discover a lie. "No. We have a basement, a wine cellar. I make the wine myself, from the grapes I grow in my garden. I have permission."

The robots pushed passed the old man, knocking him back. Anna caught her grandfather and helped him to his seat as the robots descended the stairwell to the cellar.

Light beams glowed from their eyes, turning the dark basement into daytime. There were only large casks, nothing else.

Suddenly their arms lifted, and their laser rifles slid into place. With a wide arc they circled the room, blasting each cask. Wine spurted out from half the casks, yet the deadly rays slashed through all. Anna cried out in horror. She understood what had happened, but it was too late. There was nothing she could do.

The robots paused. Their leader turned toward the girl. "We did not detect the presence of outsiders, but our computer tapes indicated you have not yet made this year's payment for your wine-merchant license. You have been operating illegally. Tomorrow you will appear in Municipal Court number three and pay your fine. In the meantime, all illegalities have been removed."

The girl was silent, struck numb, as the robots left without another word. Wine flowed everywhere; it formed puddles around her feet. Then she heard one cask shudder and open. Johnny Storm slipped safely outside. Her eyes grew wide with astonishment.

The other casks opened. Reed Richards, Sue

151

Richards, and the orange-skinned monster called the Thing eased their way to safety. "Yer plan worked perfect, Stretch. How'd ya know?"

Reed eased a pain in his back as he answered his friend's question. "We passed through Doom's robot control room during the tour, remember? I knew the frequency he operated on. I was sure a minor adjustment in our belt radio would block out our heartbeats. Fortunately, I was right."

Anna couldn't hold her shock in any longer. "They shot you. How did you live? I saw them use their terrible rays. I *saw* it."

"Each of us," Reed began, "has special powers. You must know that by now. Sue's force field protected her." Reed nodded toward Johnny. "The Human Torch's flame helped to deflect the light beams. I was able to stretch out of the way, anticipating their moves, which wasn't as difficult as you might suppose." They stared at him, confused. Reed grinned. "There was a small hole in the cask. I saw where they were aiming and shifted my body to the opposite side."

"As fer me, there ain't no laser built that can put the ol' kibbosh on yer's truly." The Thing grinned a wide, toothless grin that seemed distinctly out of place. Behind them they heard Johnny begin to giggle, then laugh, then convulse. "What's so funny, hot-head?"

It took more than a minute for Johnny to control himself, to clear the tears from his eyes. "You know why you survived, Benjamin, my orange buddy? You know why? The blamed robot missed you, that's why. But if you want to see what the laser hit, take a peek behind you."

Ben turned his massive head, and if it were possible for his orange-hued body to turn red, it would have. He backed into the corner, behind a cask still emptying its wine. The others saw his consternation. Then Sue noticed the reason and she broke into fits of laughter.

Ben was fit to be tied. "Awright! Awright! So what's so funny, lady? Ya never seen a orange butt before? Sheesh! Hey, wot're ya all starin' at me fer? Ain't ya got no courtesy? C'mon, get movin'. Get movin'!"

Laughing, Reed turned to Anna. "You wouldn't have any material we could alter for Ben, would you? I think my friend here is a bit embarrassed."

Ben squarked. "This is another one I owe Doom fer. Burnin' off my britches! That's a new low, even fer him!"

It took fifteen minutes before the laughter stopped.

෴෴෴෴෴෴෴෴෴෴෴෴෴෴෴෴෴෴෴෴෴෴෴෴෴෴෴෴

23

A green glow filled the massive wall-screen, leaving Dr. Doom speechless as he peered deeper and deeper into the strange, undescribable universe revealed before him. Alien shapes stretched into infinity, weird, crag-like formations jutted out in all directions, and then there was the vast emptiness, the long stretches of green melting into blue, fading into red and into black.

Crimson clouds floated freely through the void, wisping past multicolored dots of light: planets man had never before seen, worlds no living life forms had ever set foot upon.

This was the Negative Zone, the cosmic field of reverse polarity that Reed Richards had discovered months before and had only lately begun to explore. Doom was overwhelmed by the incredible sights he witnessed: the vast panorama of a totally alien dimension. This mind-numbing discovery had always eluded him; the piercing of another dimension had been his dream, and he had failed miserably at making that dream a reality.

But Reed Richards had pierced the cosmic plane; he alone had uncovered the secret of negative force. And though Doom cursed his foe, despised his own failure, still what he had always sought was now here within his grasp. The Negative Zone was his to harness.

He reached for the coupling units. He had to enter this Negative Zone. He had to witness firsthand its awesome power. And more, he had to siphon its negative energy, to draw it into his armor, which had been especially prepared for this very moment; the unbridled energy he needed to complete his vast cosmic scheme.

His years of planning, hoping, having his hopes dashed, re-scheming, and re-plotting were finally on the threshold of realization. Very soon the one truth that had always eluded him would be his.

The coupling unit to the Negative Zone door was melted over. Beneath his armored mask, Doom sneered. His hand grasped the adamantium steel door, electrical energy crackled from his gauntlet, and the coupling began to melt anew.

His heart beat faster; his perspiration increased. Doom felt elated, light-headed, giddy. Success was within his grasp. The steel dripped down the door like rain on a windowpane. He could hear himself breathing heavily in anticipation. Any moment now, any moment and he would fling open the door and an entirely new universe would be his.

"Hold it, Doom. You've gone far enough."

Doom knew the voice and he cursed his foe even before he turned around.

Reed Richards stood grim-faced behind him. Behind Richards was the lumbering Thing, Susan Richards, the Invisible Girl, and Johnny Storm, the Human Torch.

"You bumbling, insignificant dolts!" Doom shouted, displaying an almost insane hatred of this foursome. "I cannot be stopped now, not while I stand here ready to realize all my dreams!"

Even as he spoke, his hands danced with electrical fire. Within moments the small lab room was filled with a fearsome static charge. But Richards only shook his head sadly. "It won't help you, Doom. Our costumes are constructed from unstable molecules. Your tricks won't stop us now."

Doom's iron face-mask seemed to take on a demonic bent. Bolts of raw energy poured from his fingertips. "You contemptible fools! Don't you understand that I will not be defeated? This is the day I have awaited all my life. Nothing will go wrong. Nothing can go wrong."

The Fantastic Four moved apart from each other. Sue, Ben, and Johnny waited for Reed's command. They were a well-oiled fighting team; they knew how each of them fought, and they learned through the years how to work together like no other four people had ever done before.

At the same moment Reed Richards stretched toward Doom, his arms snaking around the master villain, Ben Grimm leaped forward and grabbed Doom's green tunic with his massive orange hand. Johnny Storm flamed on and circled over Doom, ready for any action, as Sue Richards stood back, her force field prepared to encircle Doom in an instant should Reed need her help.

Doom's hands lashed out, and they grabbed the Thing's face even as Ben's hands began to crush Doom's armor. "How dare you touch me, you misanthropic monster? For that you will perish."

Instantly, Ben's face began to freeze, and ice formed around his eyes and nose, then spread across his mouth. "What in Sam Hill are ya doin' ta me, tin-head?" Ben shivered. He released Doom from his powerful grip and clawed at the ice covering his face. "I can't breathe! Ya blasted rust-spot—yer killin' me!"

Doom laughed. "You had better believe that, you

lumbering lummox. I will destroy you as I will all your friends."

Reed's hands pulled Doom away from Ben, forcing the iron Monarch to the floor of the Baxter Building. "Johnny, help Ben—now, before it's too late. Sue, use your force field—surround Doom, isolate him."

Johnny dived toward the fallen figure of Ben Grimm. He could hear Ben choking through the thick coat of ice that surrounded his face. "Hold on, you big ox. I'll melt this gunk off you."

He doused his flame; only his hands glowed red with heat. His burning fingers touched the ice and it melted instantly. Ben shook his head weakly, gulping for breath.

"Thanks, junior. I owe ya one, but don't expect me ta pay."

Johnny grinned. "Just remember me in your will, blue-eyes."

Ben snorted. "Don't hold yer breath, hot-shot."

With a powerful backhand, Doom slammed Reed away from him. He saw Sue Richards poised, her temple throbbing. He only had a moment to act before her force field would surround him, entrap him.

He fired a shock wave at Sue's feet. She tumbled and fell backward into the small computer bank that lined the far wall. Sparks shot out in every direction as Sue crumpled to the floor.

Doom whirled and fired another blast at Reed, but the master scientist leaped backward toward another wall and reshaped his elastic body into a ball which richocheted off the wall and back into Doom. Then Reed flattened himself, and like a sheet he covered Doom completely, while his fingers probed the incredible iron armor for any weak spots. But there were none to be found anywhere.

Once more Doom electrified his armor, but this time he centered a concentrated blast at Reed's exposed face. Richards yelped with sudden pain, then fell back.

Doom lunged forward toward the Negative Zone couplings, but he was suddenly caught within a wall of fire which sprang up from nowhere. Above him he could see the Human Torch, poised and angry. "All right, Doom, you can't escape. Why not just give up and make this easy on all of us?"

Doom thrust his hands forward and fired a blast of cold air at the flaming Human Torch. "Never, you doltish clod! Doom will never surrender—not when he is so very close to final victory!"

The cold air stunned Johnny Storm. His flame ebbed, then faded, and then he fell.

Ben Grimm ran under him, his hands outstretched. "Don't worry it, junior. I got ya—though I don't know what I'm gonna *do* with ya."

Doom's hands grabbed the Negative Zone door and he pulled with all his power. The door creaked, whined, protested, but it opened a fraction, and that was more than enough.

The room was suddenly bathed in green as the door flashed open. Doom's eyes grew wide with wonderment; then his scientific curiosity turned to horror.

He found himself lifted off the floor like a leaf in the wind. The pressure grew all about him. He was unable to find a handhold as he was sucked through the door into the green vastness beyond. Behind him he saw his foes also fall victim to the incredible suction.

They were helpless, buffeted about in the stormy seas of a totally alien dimension. Doom could see the Negative Zone door move farther and farther away from him as he fell and twirled and was drawn to the center of the Zone.

Reed Richards opened his eyes and instantly he knew they were all doomed. Helpless, they were being drawn to the core of the Negative Zone, the magnetic center composed of pure negative energy.

But what frightened Reed the most was the knowledge that the moment any of these five out-of-control humans reached that central core, as their positive energy joined with the negative force, the entire Negative Zone would be completely destroyed in an explosion that could quite possibly annihilate every living being on the Earth itself.

Reed saw the Zone door still opened in the far distance. There would be no way to prevent the dimension-searing blast from escaping and taking the Earth along with it.

Helpless, tumbling head over heels, these five knew they just might soon witness the end of all life everywhere. The thought did not sit well.

24

𝕊𝕊𝕊𝕊𝕊𝕊𝕊𝕊𝕊𝕊𝕊𝕊𝕊𝕊𝕊𝕊𝕊𝕊𝕊𝕊𝕊𝕊𝕊𝕊𝕊𝕊𝕊𝕊

Doom arced forward and Reed saw a stream of smoke appear from under his long green cape. *Blast! He has a jet pack. I should have realized he'd be prepared for this. He's been waiting for this moment, waiting to do whatever it is he's planned.*

Reed watched as Doom alighted on a floating asteroid. Then he removed his cape and spread his arms upward toward the center of the Negative Zone. Tiny suction devices lined Doom's armor; intricate circuitry crisscrossed his chest beneath his tunic. *Good Lord, he's absorbing the negative energy—that's a "power drainer" he's wearing.*

The iron Monarch laughed. "You understand what I'm doing, Richards?" he shouted at the tumbling figure rushing past him. "Do you understand? I needed to tap this dimension's power. I've reconstructed my armor for this very moment. Even as we speak, even as you rush headlong to your death, negative power is being absorbed into my power condensers. I feel my strength increase, my very body changing, growing."

"It isn't gonna grow for long, Doc." The Human Torch unfurled half a dozen fireballs at Doom as he fought the tremendous suction grabbing him.

He would get Doom, stop the iron madman, then find a way back into the Baxter Building.

But Doom was ready. His fingers were spread apart and the air pulsed around him. The fireballs skidded off the energy shield Doom created. "You are a moron, child. This negative energy has given me powers you cannot even dream of. There is nothing I cannot do. Observe, you dolt—observe!"

He held his hands high, then asteroids suddenly altered course and circled Doom. He began to grow; he was more than one hundred feet tall when he paused and stared into his iron palm. Light danced across his fingers, changing shape, forming duplicates of the Fantastic Four. "With my new cosmic powers I can recreate life . . ." suddenly the figures burst into flame, then withered, ash slipping through his fingers—". . . and I can destroy that life just as simply."

Doom glanced at Ben, falling toward the destructive core. A glow surrounded the orange monster, then faded, leaving not the powerful Thing in its place, but the slimmer, human, Benjamin Grimm. "You despise your monstrous body, Grimm. It makes you little more than a mindless beast. It keeps you from the woman you love. 'How could a monster marry a human?' you cry to yourself each night. With little more than a thought, I can make you human once more. I can make your miserable life happy. You could return to your loved one not as a lumbering monstrosity, but as a human . . . as a man."

Ben Grimm gasped. It had been years since he was human, since he had become the Thing. And Doom was right—it was only his monstrous orange hide that kept him from proposing to the blind Alicia Masters . . . kept the two of them from finding happiness. But now—now he was human again. Now he—his flesh faded; it turned pink, then orange. His skin hardened, became thick, brickish. He was no longer Ben Grimm. He was the Thing again, and he was mad as hell.

"Why'd ya do that, ya slimy little filth? Why'd ya make me this monster again? If I gotta die, lemme die like a man!"

Doom's voice was like a madman's: shrill, oblivious to his surroundings. "I want you to suffer, monster. I want you all to suffer. I want you to feel pain, to know failure, to realize you will soon die and there is absolutely nothing you can do to—". Doom paused; his eyes grew narrow. "NO! The Negative energy is changing me . . . taking over my mind. It would have driven me mad, but now I have mastered it. You four will simply go to your destruction, while I leave this dimension, and wield this energy as I had long planned."

Reed saw Doom rise from the asteroid and fly back toward the Baxter Building portal. He breathed a sigh of relief. Doom would shut the door behind him. When the Negative Zone exploded, at least the Earth would be safe.

He wished he had time to explore this dimension to unravel its mysteries, to probe its special properties. On his scanner he had seen worlds populated by strange alien creatures. There was so much he could learn, so many cosmic secrets to unlock yet there was no time. Soon they would all be dead. Soon this dimension would be destroyed. It was such an utter waste.

Johnny's voice pulled Reed from his thoughts. "I think I can fight the force, Reed. If I can just get some push, that's all I need."

"Lemme toss the matchstick, Stretch. I used ta be a great pitcher back in my little-league days."

"What can I do, darling?" Sue asked. She desperately wanted to be next to Reed. If she was to die, she wanted to die alongside the man she loved.

"There may be a way, Johnny. It's risky, but it's the only chance we've got. Ben, I'm going to stretch between two of these asteroids. You pull me back like a slingshot. Johnny, I'll stretch into a pouch shape, then you douse your flame, and fit inside the pocket I form. Sue, use your force field to surround Johnny. It might not eliminate the gravity pull on him, but it will reduce the pressure. It may make it possible for him to get close enough to the Baxter Building portal to flame on and make it all the way back. Once there we can communicate by radio. Got that?"

All three nodded as Reed stretched into position. It was more than three hundred feet between the hurtling asteroids, a greater distance than Reed had ever stretched before. He wasn't sure he could make it, yet he said nothing. He had to try, even if it tore him apart. At least one would be safe. And once safe, Johnny could rescue the others.

He stretched, farther and farther. At last his hands gripped the far asteroid. He was in place, but he could feel his back aching. His arms were weak. He didn't know if he could hold on for long. Pain cut through him, but he wouldn't give in. "All right, Johnny, fly in, then flame off. I don't want you burning me."

Johnny increased the flame behind him, rocketing him toward Reed's outstretched body. He counted the seconds. Five . . . four . . . three . . . two . . . He doused his flame and a moment later Reed caught him. "All right, Ben, get behind me, and pull me back as far as you can. Sue, cover Johnny with your force shield"

Ben pulled Reed backward, bracing his legs on the asteroid. He didn't see Reed wince with pain, didn't see his friend lose consciousness. He continued to pull back, wondering how long it would be before Reed cried out. But the leader of the Fantastic Four said nothing. "Awright, ya ready, kid?" Ben waited for an answer.

Johnny shouted back toward the Thing. "Yeah. See if you can get a hole in one, Ben. I don't think we have the time for another try."

Ben released his grip, and Reed snapped forward. Johnny shot out, curving his body slightly to correct his path. The door was rushing toward him. He felt himself slowing down; the initial momentum was wearing off. He kept his eyes forward, but shouted out as loudly as he was able. "All right, Sis, lower your shield—*NOW!*"

Instantly, he flamed on and fired all his energy behind him. Once again he shot forward like a rocket. The door was directly ahead of him now. Doom had closed it: he would have to melt a hole through—it was the only way, his only hope.

He paused. concentrated, then lifted his arms before him. *Wait a second,* he thought. *If I blast open the door, I won't be able to shut it again. There's gotta be another way.*

The lock—I'll burn through the lock. I can always reseal it after they're safe. The lock melted and the door swung open again. Johnny flew on through and welded the door shut behind him. "Just hold it tight . . . tight enough for now, yet loose enough to blast it open to let the others through. We'll permanently reseal it when everyone's safe."

Johnny flicked the radio control on his belt. "I'm safe, Reed." He waited for an answer, but for a moment there wasn't any. Then Sue's voice came over the receiver. "Reed's unconscious, Johnny.

The strain must have been too much for him. But thank goodness *you're* safe."

Then Ben's voice crackled over the radio. "Kid, ya gotta find us some kinda rope or somethin' ta grab onta. Send it through that doohickey Reed set up ta explore the Neg Zone without openin' the door."

Johnny smiled. "Good idea, big man. Hold on tight, will ya? I'll be right back."

He ran through the lab door to the stairwell. "*FLAME ON!*" he shouted. There wasn't time for the elevator. He had to fly up to the next level, then get inside the storage room and find some heavy cables.

A moment later he was back before the Negative Zone computers. "I'm here, Ben. Is everyone all right?"

"Sure, sure. We always get off on hurtlin' ta our deaths. C'mon, punk. Move yer butt."

Johnny's hand reached for the computer, and his fingers danced over the controls. He had seen Reed work these dials a dozen times. He knew them by heart.

Using the controls, he could create a small opening to the Negative Zone, connected to the computer by an equally narrow airlock. Johnny could then feed the cable through the computer and it would emerge somewhere in the Zone. Using the scalar grid on the computer terminal, he could arrange it to appear by the entrance back into the Baxter Building.

At the same time Johnny knew the cable would be drawn to the Negative Zone core just as Reed, Ben, and Sue were. But it, being lighter, would soon overtake them. They, in turn, could grab the cable, and Johnny, using a hoist, could draw them back home.

If it worked, of course, and Johnny wasn't sure it would. They never had to use pinpoint accuracy in the Zone before, and without such accuracy, his teammates would surely die.

Johnny shut his eyes and activated the airlock. On the viewscreen he could see the cable unfurl, one end still in the Baxter Building, the other unwinding into the Negative Zone.

"The creep did it, Susie! He did it!" Ben was shouting with joy as the cable floated toward them. Reed was still unconscious in Ben's arms. *Why didn't he say he was hurtin'? 'Cause he didn't want us ta make 'im stop. He knew if we suspected he was in pain, we'd never've let 'im go through with it. Reed may be a big-talkin' scientist who seems kinda cold now an' then, but the guy has a heart that just never stops.*

"Ben!" Sue's voice was filled with horror. Then Ben saw the reason why. The cable was veering off, away from them. They wouldn't be able to catch it.

Ben shot a glance at Reed. If he were conscious, there would be no trouble. He could stretch to the cable, bring it to them, but he was barely breathing.

Then Ben saw Sue move. Her temple was glowing. Although he was unable to see her send out an invisible coil of force, he knew what she was doing. He watched the cable suddenly twist toward them, as if grabbed by an invisible hook. "Susie, yer a dream gal. Ya did it." He remembered the early days of the Fantastic Four. Sue had often wondered if she contributed her share to the team. Her powers of invisibility seemed useless. But since those early days she had learned to harness her force field, and now she was probably the most powerful member of them all.

"C'mon, Sis, grab the cable." Johnny was shouting into the radio as he watched the drama unfold. He saw her stretch out a hand and bring the cable to her. Ben Grimm leaped off his asteroid and grabbed the cable in one hand, still holding Reed with the other.

"All right, hold tight. I'm using a winch. You should be safe in a few minutes."

Johnny watched as they floated closer to him. He could see the stress on their faces. The terrible forces within the Negative Zone still lashed out against them. It took all their strength to grasp the cable and not let go.

They were coming closer. Johnny strapped himself to a steel post, then tied steel cord around it, the other end ready to lasso Ben and Sue as the Neg-Zone door opened. They were by the outside portal now.

Once more he blasted open the door. It flew open, and an overwhelming force cut through the room. Johnny felt himself being drawn into the Zone, but he was held tight to the post. Unknown energy contorted his face as he shouted. "Grab the cords . . . tie them around you, then pull yourself in! When you're safe I'll shut the door again. Just hurry! *HURRY!*"

Sue faltered, and her fingers slipped from the cable, but Ben caught her with his free hand while gripping the cable with his legs. "C'mon, Susie, ya ain't gonna go fallin' back inta that mess after all o' this."

Sue shouted to be heard over the roar of energy whipping past her. "I can't hold on, Ben! I haven't got the strength! Save yourself and Reed! Forget about me!"

Ben shook his head violently. "No way, lady. I save us all, or I don't save any of us. Got that? Ya

168

want yer hubby breathin' again, ya gotta try 'n' pull yerself in, too."

Through the portal Ben could see Johnny. He was helpless, tied to that post. If anyone had to make a move, it was up to Ben, but both his hands were tied. "Awright, lissen ta me, Susie. I'm holdin' onta ya real tight. See if ya can slip that cord around yerself and Stretcho. If ya can, I can toss ya back inside. Then I'll follow. Got that?"

Sue nodded, saying nothing. She could barely think. Her hands reached out and grabbed the cords. She pulled one around her; the other she tied to Reed. "All right, Ben. I've done it. Now what?"

Ben said nothing as he threw back his massive shoulders, then pitched Sue forward as if she were little more than a baseball. Reed followed a moment behind. *Good,* Ben thought. *At least they're safe. Now ta get me outta this revoltin' development.*

Arm over arm, he pulled himself along the cable. It vanished into a small hole, but the hole was alongside the gateway back to safety. If Ben could pull himself close enough, he could grab the door and drag himself through.

He felt the raw energy lash into him, sting him, whip him. He was in incredible pain, but he kept moving forward.

Suddenly the door was in front of him. His right hand grabbed the edge and he leaned forward. His left picked a handhold, and he slowly pulled himself through. "Hot head, shut the blasted door behind me, or I'll go sailin' right back out."

Johnny shouted back, trying to keep his balance in the fury of the Negative Zone wind. "Pull yourself all the way through, Ben! You're still sticking out! C'mon! Get through, you big buffoon! Hurry!"

169

Ben was through. Johnny freed himself from the post and he was forced toward the Zone door. If he didn't time this perfectly, he would go back through, never to be found. Neither Ben, Sue, nor Reed had the strength to search for him. He had to make his move now.

He reached the door and slammed it shut. The door fought to stay open, but Johnny welded it in place. Suddenly the pressure stopped and Johnny fell to the ground, his chest heaving in pain, his lungs desperate for air.

He allowed himself to rest for a moment. Then he completed the welding job. The door to the Negative Zone was sealed, and Johnny thanked God for that.

He didn't want to go through hell ever again.

꙳꙳꙳꙳꙳꙳꙳꙳꙳꙳꙳꙳꙳꙳꙳꙳꙳꙳꙳꙳꙳꙳꙳꙳꙳꙳꙳꙳꙳꙳꙳꙳꙳꙳

25

Victor Von Doom stood silent and pensive beside the massive thirty-five-ton Heelstone, his grim gaze riveted on the great trilithon seventy-five meters away. Night still blanketed the great plains of Salisbury, and the moon, low on the far horizon, made the awesome monoliths of Stonehenge a black silhouette painted on a dark gray canvas.

To the East, Doom could see the sun begin to rise; golden glimmers of light made hesitant intrusions into the blackness everywhere. It was now time. Before the sun was high, when it could still be seen stretching across the long, endless plains, Doom had to position himself before the double trilithon, the four massive stone pillars topped with three stone slabs.

Then, as the sun rose from behind the Heelstone, and light pierced the spaces between the trilithons, he would utter the words he had read so many years before in his mother's diary. The spaces between the columns would then shimmer with an alien glow, and Doom would unleash the energy he had tapped from the dark recesses of the Negative Zone. Then, at long last, he would have what he had long prayed for. He would pierce the veil between life and death itself. He would enter the forbidden regions of the netherverse; he would cross into the shadow zone where those long dead still walked.

Through this region he would seek out the one he wanted. He would find Cynthia, his long-departed mother. He would speak to this woman he was so much like, yet had never truly known. And he would learn from her the darkest secrets that had always eluded his grasp.

Around him were the remains of Stonehenge, the last vestiges of a people who lived more than four thousand years before; not the Druids, as man had long suspected, but of three separate tribes, each changing, each adding to make Stonehenge the mystic monument it was.

Doom kneeled by the great trilithon and the three windows into the netherworld. From his cloak he removed the old book of spells he had found as a child in his father's trunk. And though he had long ago memorized the words, he opened to the proper page and read the prayer written so many years before in the hand of his mother.

The stones were black against a golden light as he raised his hands toward the heavens. "Astoreth and Mogoleth, Shintath and Beelzebub, demons of darkness and light, shadows and substance, reality and fantasy, truth and lies, I, who am worthless, call upon your powers great and terrible. I humble myself before your greatness. I sacrifice myself before your wonderment. I am nothing and you are all."

The chasms of light between the stones grew dark and scarlet. Doom raised his head and saw the sunlight filtering in everywhere but between these four great stones. The spell was working. Soon he would find his mother. Soon she would tell him the spells that would give him the power over every living being on Earth.

Doom stood between the center stones, his hands outstretched, touching the portal walls. He could see into the scarlet, see the dark shimmering shapes trudge slowly here and about, as if weighted down by anchors.

He could see the outlines of ten million figures, then ten million more. All who had ever died were here before him now. He could reach out and touch a Caesar, or a Napoleon, or an Einstein, should he choose to do so. But he wished to speak to only one soul. He wanted his mother.

His fingers glowed as the negative energy he had tapped poured from his armor. It would cut a path through the shadow region. He could use it to open the dimension as he had never been able to open it before. He could enter the land of the dead, walk beside the souls and find his mother's essence. At last he could penetrate the lands beyond.

The scarlet haze seemed to part, and for the first time Doom could see the region beyond as clearly as if it were real and shared his substance. No longer was it a misty unknown. No longer was it impenetrable. Now it belonged to him.

Dr. Doom had mastered the land of the dead.

And then he stepped within.

Time flowed backward here. Those most recently deceased stepped in slow motion before him. He would have to penetrate the veil even deeper. He would have to go back those many years to the time when he was still an infant.

Negative energy crackled around him with every step forward he took. He passed bodies he had known, others that he recognized; most he could care less about. They were simply dead ones not to be bothered with.

His step was slow and precise; he had to stay on his path or he could never leave this land of the shadows.

Then, like something muffled by cotton, he heard a distant voice. It called his name. "Doom . . . Doom!" He looked about, but there was no one before him he recognized. The voice became louder, more penetrating.

He realized it wasn't coming from within this veiled dimension. It came from outside, back in Stonehenge. Suddenly everything vanished and he was standing before the trilithon. Behind him, the sun to their backs, stood the Fantastic Four.

Reed ran toward him. "Don't do it, Doom. You'll unleash forces you can't control."

Doom's eyes were wide in shock. "How did you find me? How did you know?"

"You absorbed radiation and energy from the Negative Zone. Long ago, when I first learned of the Zone's existence, I created a detector for that energy. It was a simple matter to adjust it to follow you. With that power coursing through you, you were like a radar beacon."

"Then you followed me here only to die. I shall not fail, Richards. Not now. I swear that."

Doom shimmered with wild, crackling energy. "I've enough power to reopen the gateway, and still enough to keep you away from me while I do."

"Stand back, everyone!" Reed shouted as he ducked behind a column.

Sue spread her energy field around her, and Johnny flamed on and flew high over the stone monoliths. Only Ben Grimm stood in place, his fists waving at Doom.

174

"Ya crummy little tin can, I'm fed up ta here with ya. Ya try 'n' kill us, ya do everythin' ya want ta destroy us. But ya didn't succeed, Doomsie, ya didn't win, an' ya won't win—'cause we're the ever-lovin' Fantastic Four. An' mister, we got the power ta lay you low!"

Doom was frothing at the mouth, his voice raised to a fevered pitch. His eyes crackled with unbridled energy. "You insignificant little cretin, you fail to understand the power I now control. You cannot possibly comprehend the magnificence of my discovery. I possess powers undreamed of. I have seen the other side; I have crossed the vale into the land of the dead. And you actually have the tenacity to say you are going to stop me from completing that which I've only begun?

"Dolt! Ludicrous, moronic dolt—not even you possess that power. No one but Doom possesses the power." His hands raised, his feet spread apart, the field of energy surrounding Doom began to spread wide and out.

It pushed through the other monoliths, and like the ripples in a pond continued to radiate outward from the center. Ben stepped toward the sparkling black cloud that swirled before him. He reached out to touch it. Instantly, he felt himself on fire. His hand grew numb; he froze as the cloud swept over him. His body was burning up. At any moment he would ignite and instantly crumble to ash.

"Ben! Get out of there!" Johnny swooped downward but saw Reed Richards wave him away.

"Don't, Johnny—if you touch him you'll be affected, as well. Sut, throw a skintight force field around me. It's Ben's only chance."

Sue nodded and complied. A moment later Reed stretched toward Ben. He wrapped his elongated body around the orange-hided Thing from head to

175

foot, then stretched toward a distant monolith. With all his strength he snapped his body forward, and Ben was whisked back, away from the field.

Reed shouted toward Johnny, who landed at his side. "Quickly, use your powers—siphon away the heat. If we can lower his body temperature before it causes any permanent damage, Ben has a chance of surviving."

Johnny grabbed Ben's arms and closed his eyes. "Ya gotta live, big buddy. Man, ya gotta live."

Sue held onto Reed's arm as they both watched the red glow that surrounded Ben begin to fade. Johnny was doing it. He was siphoning off the searing heat which was killing Ben.

As Ben collapsed to the ground, the others clustering about him, Dr. Doom turned once more to the trilithon. For a second time the sacred words were spoken, and again the scarlet haze filtered through the three portals.

He stepped inside, no longer content to gaze in wonderment. About him on all sides were the walking dead. He continued on through, passing the wretched and the worthless, pushing aside the useless and those who served not his purpose.

"Victor?" He heard the voice call him. Was it a trick? Was it that infernal Reed Richards *again*? He continued on and the voice grew louder. "Victor." The voice was dark, ethereal, strange beyond recognition. Yet it came from within the land of the shadow. He pushed forward.

He stood before the man who smiled at him. "Victor, I knew one day you would come here, my son."

"Father?" Doom stared at him, unsure what to say. "Father? I do not believe it. It can't be you."

"Why not?" the man answered calmly. "You came to the land of the dead. I am dead. You

176

seek your mother, but I died more recently. It is only correct that you must pass me before you can reach your goal."

"You know why I am here, Father?"

"You seek power, Victor. I know that. I have always known that, and I have always prayed you would not find it."

"What? You want me to be a weak-kneed fool like the others? No, Father. You have changed. Or perhaps you forget how the Baron's men killed my mother. Perhaps you forget that we fled from their tyranny, and you died because of them. But I have not forgotten that, Father. And I seek my absolute power to destroy all those who have both hunted and feared Von Doom."

Werner Von Doom grew angry, his face contorted in the eerie glow. "No, Victor, it is you who have forgotten the truth. I always sought to help people. I would never raise a finger to cause any man harm. Your mother was the same, Victor. She used her powers for good, not evil. No, my son, we have not changed. You have. You have become evil, twisted. You are no longer my son."

"You lie, old man!" Doom was shouting now, his face livid with hatred. He wanted to throttle the old one but found he could not. "All my life I sought vengeance on those who killed my parents. Now you dare to call me mad. Never! Never!"

Arrogantly, Doom pushed his father, but the older man would not move. "Do not stop me, Father. I want to see my mother. I want to hear the dark prayers from her lips."

"She will not teach them to you, Victor. She, too, abhors what you have become. Accept the truth, Victor—return to your world and change

177

your ways. There is time. There is always time while you still live."

Doom raised his hands high; bolts of negative energy formed in a circle around them. "You are telling me that everything I have ever dreamed of is a lie, everything I have ever strived for is false. No! That cannot be. That must never be. No man, not even you, can tell me that!"

The negative force expanded. It enveloped Doom and spread to his father and cut through the scarlet haze that was everywhere. Doom's voice, strong and powerful, became distant and muffled. "Everything cannot be a lie. I sought power for vengeance . . . now vengeance cannot be mine . . . no . . . no . . . I cannot accept that . . . I—"

"You are wrong, Victor; you sought your vengeance not for us, but for yourself. You wanted powers that should belong to no man. You make me ashamed that you were born of our flesh. Renounce your evil ways, Victor. Renounce them, or we shall renounce you."

"Never, you weak-kneed old fool. If I was wrong about anything, it was my love for you. You were always a fool. A strong man would have fought back when the Baron killed his wife. But you, oh, you permitted him his fun. You said nothing as my mother died. Now, out of my way, Father, or, so help me, I'll blast you where you stand."

"Then do so, Victor. I will not move." His father lowered his hands to his side and Doom raised his armored hand and unleashed a terrible destructive ray at the man he had worshipped for so many years.

The man crumpled to the ground, and Doom stepped past the spot where his father had stood a moment before. *The contemptible fool. He was wrong about everything. But I still seek my mother. She will show me the way. She will tell me how Dr. Doom can rule this world.*

The path before him was long and winding and it threatened to go on forever into the distance. But that mattered none to Dr. Doom. Nothing mattered to him now except the finding of his mother. She will help him. She will guide him to his ultimate triumph.

After all, she had named him Victor. How could victory elude him?

He continued along the path, disgusted at the peasants who walked somnambulistically beside him. What foul creatures these are, he felt. They were not fit to walk the same path his mother walked.

He saw her in the distance; her long white gown shimmered against the pale red mist. He called out to her. "Mother?" She turned, and he saw she was as beautiful as he had been told.

"Mother? Is that you?" Silently, she nodded.

"I am Cynthia Von Doom, Victor. You are my son, and the killer of my husband. Why have you invaded the serenity of my death? Why have you sought me out? Why do you not leave us alone? Have you not already disgraced the name Von Doom? Have you not made a mockery of all we had taught you? Leave me alone, Victor. Your father has already banished you. I do not wish to see you now, or ever. *Go!*"

"No! You cannot mean that. I, who have always called your name. I love you. I want to sit by your side and learn from you. You were a witch and I inherited your awesome power. Surely you cannot renounce my destiny—a destiny that you, yourself, created."

Her eyes flared with fire as she spoke. "To be

a witch is not to be evil. It is to possess power, and power can be used for good. You choose to use your power for evil, Victor. You made your decision yourself. Do not pretend that I gave you that legacy. Do not believe I wish you to be as you are.

"Look at yourself, Victor. Look at your face."

Doom saw a silver mirror appear before him and his mask mystically opened. He saw the scarred battleground his face had become: a twisted, disgusting mockery of humanity. His hands flew to his face, he covered his ravaged features with his palms, but still the haunting visage appeared in the mirror. Still he could see his evil persona stare back at him in horror.

"You are as twisted and evil as your face, Victor. You have permitted yourself to die long before death had ever claimed you. Now, Victor, renounce your past. Now, Victor, change your ways. There may yet be time for salvation. Speak, my son. Tell the gods you wish to be a new man. Shout to all who can hear that Victor Von Doom is dead, and a phoenix shall rise from his ashes. Speak now, or forever face damnation."

Doom's bloodshot eyes were wide in horror as he stared at the woman he knew to be his mother. "You ask me things I cannot do. You should know that I am Victor Von Doom. I cannot surrender myself to such beliefs. No, mother, if you are truly her, and if this shadow land has not changed you, as it has my father, then you would honor me as I am. You would acknowledge that I have fought to be worthy of the name Von Doom.

"Our name was once spat upon by the Barons of Latveria. Now it is a name to be feared and respected. You cannot tell me I am evil, for I have read your diary. I know how you once thought. I spoke your dark spells as you once had. I am your son; you cannot deny me that."

"Victor, I spoke those spells as a child. But long before I met your father, I renounced the ways of the black witches and dark sabbats. That diary was mine, kept to remind me of my awesome power and the evil it could cause. I relinquished that power. You embraced it. I am sorry, Victor, truly I am sorry. But there is no further use for us to talk.

"I cannot permit you to return to your land of the living and to wield your terrible power. I cannot allow you to wreck havoc on an unsuspecting mankind. You must remain here, where our forces will change you. You will see the truth, Victor. You will accept the truth as all men come to do."

Doom stepped back, his hands outstretched, waving away the woman who approached him. He pushed through two walking corpses, and ran terrified along the narrow path. His mother followed behind him, walking slowly, yet never falling far behind.

Doom ran, his hopes, his dreams, all shattered. He damned his mother and father, and cursed this land of shadows, and knew he could stay here not a moment more. "I have mastered death!" he cried. "You will not master me!"

He turned as he ran. His mother was still behind him, arms beckoning him toward her. "Stay here, Victor. It is your only chance. If you return to your world, you will face horrors unknown to man. Remain here with us."

He whirled and fired a terrifying blast at the beckoning figure. His mother smiled as the golden glow surrounded her. "I am already dead, Victor. I cannot die again."

"No more than I could die, Victor." Once more Doom spun, and he saw Werner Von Doom standing before him. "There was no way for me to hold you, my son. You had to see the truth. Your mother had to be the one to show it to you."

"No! You lie! You all lie!" Doom slammed his hand into his father, but the man did not move. Sweat beaded down Doom's face, stinging his still sore wounds.

"Allow your mother to hold you, Victor. You will learn."

Doom struggled, but his father held him still. He saw his mother approach him. She lifted her hand and she smiled. He screamed as her warm hand descended on his iron-clad shoulder.

Beyond the wall of seething energy, the Fantastic Four could only stand and watch. Ben Grimm stirred and rose to his feet. Doom could be seen standing in the scarlet mist. Another figure stood behind him, a smaller, slender figure before him. They could hear Doom scream and struggle, and fight.

Ben tried to reach out, but Reed called him back. "Don't—whatever is happening to Doom, we can't affect its outcome. It's not happening here. We can only observe it."

"But what is it, Reed? I don't understand?" Johnny shook his head in bewilderment.

"I don't understand it either, Johnny. I don't think any of us could hope to comprehend what's happening to him now."

Sue cried out. "Look—everything's fading . . . it's all disappearing. It's as if it's all over.

"And Doom's being taken away—the mist's covering him—he's looking back at us, Reed. Look at him—look at his face. He's calling to us. Reed!

He wants our help. He wants us to grab him. Can't we do anything, Reed?"

Reed shook his head. "No, Sue. This is beyond even our power. Doom unleashed forces that cannot be controlled. And now he's paying the ultimate penalty."

The scarlet mist covered Doom in a shroud of darkness. Suddenly the glow from the trilithon seemed to expand beyond the gateway. Crimson bolts shot out in all directions as the wind whipped through the Stonehenge monuments.

Reed cried out. "Grab onto a boulder—this is all coming to a head!"

Suddenly Stonehenge was caught in the throes of a hurricane. Johnny felt his body being torn from the stone he grabbed onto. Reed tied his legs about his massive monolith and stretched toward his young teammate. "Sue! We need you now—try to encircle us with a force bubble."

The scarlet shroud seemed to blanket all of Stonehenge. Then, suddenly, there was nothing. The winds fell silent, and they saw the crimson color fade and sunlight stream through the trilithon. The dimension of shadows was gone, and it had taken Dr. Doom with it.

Reed fell to the ground weak, panting for breath. In the distance he could hear a tour bus turning into the parking lot across the highway. In a few minutes the first tourists of the day would come streaming over the Salisbury Plain, snapping photographs, gaping at the ages-old monument, wondering who had built it and what purpose it had served.

A few would see four tired, haggard figures stagger from the ruins and enter a private car which would soon take them to a distant airport.

But none would ever know what had transpired here just moments before.

And another mystery of Stonehenge would be swallowed up by time.

26

Anna sipped her tea and listened as Johnny spoke. It was difficult to listen to the handsome young American, for her heart was leaping with joy at the news he revealed.

"We don't know what happened to Doom. He just vanished within the mist. But he's gone, and I guess that means your people are now free."

Erich stood by the window, watching his fellow Latverians pass by outside, passing the word of Doom's disappearance one to the other. He could sense a reluctant happiness out there. The people were happy Doom would no longer rule them, but they were also unsure what would happen to them next. With Doom they had more food than they ever had before. He supplied them with medical facilities that were far in advance of any other nation. He had made their life simpler than had the Barons who had ruled them for centuries. And now that they were free, they wondered if they really wanted their freedom.

"The people are confused," Erich said sadly. "Latverians have not known freedom for so many years they have forgotten what the word means. Perhaps they fear they will now have to struggle to get what Doom gave them, but they will have earned their benefits; they will not have traded away their lives for a serving of vegetables. I have confidence we will succeed."

Ben lumbered into Anna's small home, slapping his hands in satisfaction. "I just polished off a couple o' Doom's robots. Now they ain't nothin' more'n a scrap heap o' junk. I just wish they coulda been Doomsie himself. Stretcho, ya think he'll ever come back?"

"I wish I knew, Ben. We only heard his part of the conversation. From everything I could garner, he had opened the door that separates life and death and then had the door slam shut behind him. Frankly, I don't know what that means. I'm not sure if he's alive, or what."

Ben grinned. "Hey, so ya ain't the big-brained genius I always thought ya wuz. That makes a gargoyle like me feel better. C'mon, why don't we split now? I wanna get back ta the Big Apple an' take Alicia out fer a big juicy steak."

"I agree with Ben, Reed." Sue walked toward the door. "I don't like leaving Franklin for days at a time. It isn't healthy for a child to grow up without his parents.

"Johnny, you coming?"

"I'll be with you in a minute, Sis. Let me just say good-bye, please." He waited until the others left. "Anna, I hope you can understand what we did and why we did it. I wanted to help your people, but I couldn't—not the way you wanted me to."

Anna put her hand to Johnny's lips. "I can understand, John Storm, and now I can even agree with you. You see, now it is up to my people to make Latveria into the land we have always wished for. If we can be a strong people, we will

186

survive. If not . . . " She allowed the thought to fade.

"But you have helped us so very much, John Storm. We will never forget you. *I* will never forget you. You have given us hope. What more could we have ever asked for?"

Without a word, Anna pressed forward and her lips touched Johnny's. He drew his arms about her, held her firm in his grasp Then they moved apart and Johnny smiled, then turned to join his friends. "Good-bye, Anna," he said simply. "I will never forget you, either."

Reed, Sue, and Ben were already in the limousine ready to take them to the airport and home when Johnny opened the door and stepped from Anna's small home.

He knocked on the door and waited. There was no answer, but he could hear the shower running upstairs and knew she would be home. He sat on the stoop and thought about the past several days, thought about Anna, thought about Frankie Raye and wondered if she would be interested in going out with him again, but no longer on her terms. He would not disguise who he was, he would not pretend his super-hero side did not exist any more than he could pretend his powers did not exist. He was who he was, and there was nothing he could or wanted to do about it. He wanted Frankie Raye, he was still in love with her, yet if she was unable to accept him without special conditions, then he would have to say good-bye, and he would be alone and not at all happy, but he would not have compromised himself. He would not have thrown away who he was to pretend he was something else.

The door opened. Frankie peered through the narrow opening and smiled at Johnny. She undid the chain and opened the door fully. "I thought I heard the bell ringing. Johnny Storm, am I ever glad it's you."

"Huh? I thought you never wanted to see me again."

Frankie Raye nodded. "You're right, I thought so, too. But I've gone mad these past few days. I've called you every hour. I went to the Baxter Building but I couldn't get inside. Johnny, oh, Johnny, I'm just so happy you came back. You didn't know what I was thinking, how I was punishing myself for everything.

"You have to understand something about me, Johnny. I get very afraid sometimes. I've been alone for too many years, and when you walked into my life I thought I'd never have to be alone again. But then, well, when I learned who you were, what you were, I knew that someday you might go out and never return, and I'd be alone, and I just wasn't able to cope with that.

"It wasn't your problem, Johnny. It's mine. And I don't know if I can change, but, oh, God, Johnny, I want to try. I don't want to lose you, and I don't want to change you into something I don't want. If you're willing, if you'll have me after everything I've said, will you come back?"

Johnny paused and said nothing. He just stared into her beautiful eyes for a long while. Then finally he grinned.

"How about a burger and some fries, kid? It's not fancy, but it's me all the way."

"That sounds good to me, Johnny Storm. Sounds just great to me."

27

Boris sat in the darkness of the castle for a very long time, rocking in the old chair his master had given him many years before. Muffled through the windows he could hear the singing in the streets, the shouting of happy people. It had been so long since he had heard his people laugh.

He thought of his master and remembered him when he was young. He was always such a bright child, yet even then his destiny could be read in his dark, brooding eyes. His end would come by his own hand. That had been the prophecy, he remembered. His great pride would ever be his downfall.

Boris forced himself to stand. Then he rested a moment on his staff before moving on. He heard the rocking chair slowly creak to a halt, and he thought he heard his name being called, but when he turned he knew the sound he had heard was only the howling wind.

At the doorway he paused to catch his breath. He smiled, remembering his master standing young and proud in his Latverian lab months before fate first brought him to America. His mother's diary was open on a table before him, his bright brown hair rolling in the gentle breeze.

"Nothing shall ever stop Victor Von Doom," he stated then. "With my diary and my resolve, all secrets will be revealed. Not even death itself will be a mystery to me. Indeed, faithful Boris, I swear to you now, the dark region of the shadows will never claim my soul. When the time comes, when the other world seeks me out, then I shall face my greatest challenge. Then I shall prove that Dr. Doom has even conquered Death itself."

Boris turned from the room and hobbled down the long stone corridor tapping his cane before him. The wind rushed through the winding hall and Boris slowly walked to the window and drew the shutters closed. He paused and wondered what he would do now, where he would go, how he would live. This castle had been his home for so many years, it would feel strange not to live here still.

All his friends had died many years before; now he was alone, old and crippled.

He left the chamber and entered his small room. From the closet he withdrew a bag. It was small and torn, but there wasn't much he wanted to take with him. He stuffed one shirt in the bag, folded in a pair of pants, and zippered the bag shut.

Wistfully, he smiled as he left the room, walking down the long corridors to the main entrance. Upon the walls were paintings of Doom: standing proud, hands on his hips, riding horses, greeting his subjects.

So tragic, so very tragic.

He paused again in the main chamber and stared at Doom's empty throne. *There will never be another like him again*, he thought. Such strength, and such arrogance. Such brilliance, and so little compassion.

Doom could have been a great man, but now he would go down in history as a villain, one of the infamous in the same league as Khan, or Hitler.

Boris heard the wind howl his name again, but the shutters were closed tight, and no curtain rippled. He thought he could see Doom sitting in his chair, his heavy iron hands outstretched, beseeching him to come closer.

Boris shook his head. *I am an old man, too old. Much too old. I should find a place to stay tonight, then lie down.*

Then he heard his name called again, softly, like a shadow's whisper.

And this time he knew he had not heard the wind.